F   JUNE   HC
LP   COPELAND, LORI   01/01
COP

	DATE DUE	
FEB 2	1098	APR 2 4 '02 1016
FEB 2 7	1181	NOV 0 3 '02 1184
MAR 1 2	1215	NOV 2 6 '02 1303
APR 3	1044	JAN 0 2 '03 1044
APR 2 0	1294	JAN 1 6 '03 1060
MAY 1 8	1021	AUG 1 4 '03 1316 1039
JUN 1 5	1091	JUN 0 2 2004 1029
JUN 2 7		AUG 1 3 2004 1370
AUG 3 1 '01	1067	SEP 0 8 2005 1370
SEP 18 '01	1067	JUL 2 5 2007 1591
SEP 26 '01	1407	MAR 1 2 2009 1458

AUG 1 8 2009 1491
NOV 2 8 2013 1642
MAY 3 0 2014 1476
AUG 2 6 2014 1476

HEART
QUEST™

HeartQuest brings you romantic fiction
with a foundation of biblical truth.
Adventure, mystery, intrigue, and suspense
mingle in our heartwarming stories of
men and women of faith striving to build
a love that will last a lifetime.

May HeartQuest books sweep you
into the arms of God, who longs for you
and pursues you always.

June

LORI COPELAND

Brides of the West 1872

BOOKSPAN LARGE PRINT EDITION

Tyndale House Publishers, Inc.
WHEATON, ILLINOIS

This Large Print Edition, prepared especially for
Bookspan, contains the complete, unabridged
text of the original Publisher's Edition.

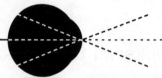

This Large Print Book carries the
Seal of Approval of N.A.V.H.

A Note from the Author

Dear Reader,

Thank you for the overwhelming response to book 1 in my Brides of the West series, *Faith*. I hope you will enjoy June Kallahan's story as she travels all the way to Seattle to marry her husband-to-be—whoever that turns out to be! Life can sometimes be unpredictable, but by keeping our eyes on Jesus Christ our Savior, we can rest in the assurance that he works all things together for our good and his glory.

Lori Copeland

Prologue

Cold Water, Michigan, late 1800s

Billows of white smoke rolled from the train's stack as a shrill whistle announced its imminent arrival. Turning to give Aunt Thalia a final hug, June Kallahan blinked back tears.

"I'll write you the moment I get settled, Aunt Thalia."

The old woman's arms tightened around June's neck, holding on longer than necessary. "I'm going to miss you, child."

"Don't worry about me," June said softly. "It's you I worry about."

"I'll be going to a better place someday very soon. No need for anyone to worry about me. But *of course* I'll worry about you. My age ought to afford me *some* rights. And I'll worry about your sisters. Faith gone off to Texas, Hope to Kentucky." Thalia Grayson shook her head. "Sakes alive. You've all taken leave of your senses."

June lovingly patted her old aunt's back. "God will take care of us, Auntie."

The engine came to a halt amid a *whoosh* of steam and squealing brakes. Passengers got off while others hurried to board. The stopover in Cold Water was brief. Smiling, June blew Aunt Thalia a final kiss as she reached for her bag. "Don't worry! I'll be fine!"

Running toward the coach, June determined to keep up her brave facade. Auntie would worry enough without sending her off in a flurry of tears. The conductor caught her hand and lifted her aboard as the train slowly pulled out of the station. Standing on the car's platform, June smiled and waved until Aunt Thalia's stooped frame faded into the distance.

Fighting her tears, June made her way into the coach, wondering if Faith and Hope had felt the same insecurities when they left, two weeks earlier.

A gentleman got up and offered his seat. Murmuring her thanks, June sat down, then buried her face in her handkerchief and bawled. Was she doing the right thing? Should she stay and take care of Auntie—let Faith and Hope be the mail-order brides? Aunt Thalia was old. Who would look after her?

The gentleman leaned forward. "Are you all right, miss?"

June wiped her tears, sitting up straighter. "Yes, thank you. I'm fine."

The enormity of what she was about to do overwhelmed her. She was off to Seattle—hundreds and hundreds of miles from Cold Water, about to marry a man she knew only by the few letters they'd exchanged.

She was about to marry Eli Messenger, and she didn't even know him.

The idea had made so much sense a few weeks ago. With their father, Thomas Kallahan, dead and Aunt Thalia unable to bear the financial responsibility of three additional mouths to feed, she and her sisters knew they must be keepers of their own fates. The decision to become mail-order brides had not been made easily, nor without a great deal of prayer.

June stared out the window, listening to the wheels clacking against the metal rails, wheels carrying her away from Cold Water to a brand-new life. She thought about her soon-to-be husband, Eli Messenger, and the unfamiliar world that awaited her in Seattle. Eli was a man of God, associate pastor to the famed Isaac Inman, of the Isaac Inman Evangelistic Crusade. Everyone had heard of Isaac Inman—of his unflagging dedication to God, his charismatic personality, how he led hundreds of thousands of lost souls to find salvation. Goose bumps rose on her arms when she thought about meeting the world-renowned minister in person. Not only would she meet Isaac Inman, but she would work beside him! Papa would be so proud of her, were he still alive.

Removing Eli's letter from her purse, she scanned the last paragraph.

Together, we will work for God's kingdom. Our life will be good, June. I know you must experience moments of doubts about your venture, but I believe God has destined us to be together, to work together for his glory. I eagerly anticipate your arrival and the beginning of what surely promises to be our wonderful life together.

She refolded the letter and tucked it safely back in her purse. Resting her head on the back of the seat, she willed herself to relax. Everything was as it should be.

Clickety-clack, clickety-clack.

Every turn of the wheel carried her farther and farther away from the only life she had ever known.

Biting down hard on her lower lip, she prayed that Eli Messenger was right and that God did, indeed, intend them for each other.

Otherwise, she was heading straight for the pits of—

She caught her wayward thoughts. She would surely, at best, be heading straight for trouble.

Chapter One

Raining again?" June Kallahan stood on tiptoe to look out the ship porthole. "Doesn't it ever let up?"

Samantha Harris pressed closer, elbowing a larger peephole in the dirty pane. "Can't allow a bit o' rain to spoil your day, lovey. Do you see your intended?"

June anxiously searched the landing area. Eli had said to look for a man, five foot ten, fair skinned, with sandy brown hair and hazel eyes. As she scanned the milling crowd, her heartbeat quickened. Where could he be?

"Do you think he'll like me, Sam?"

"Oh, 'ow could 'e *not* like you?" Sam

gave June's arm a jaunty squeeze. "You bein' so comely and all."

"Comely?" June laughed. She'd struck up an instant friendship with this charming English waif the moment they boarded ship in San Francisco. Sam was en route to Seattle to assist her ailing aunt, who ran a small orphanage. Sam's accent was pure delight—a touch of cockney and Irish brogue amid the English, with Sam's own particular manners of speech thrown in for color.

"Goodness, Sam. There isn't a comely thing about me. My nose is too long, my eyes are too close-set, and this hair! Just look at it, Sam! It's a bundle of frizz."

"Shame on ya! It's beautiful! So dark and curly. Truly, lovey, it is. And those big brown eyes o' yours are sure to melt his heart."

June gave a quick shake of her head. "The only comely daughter my papa sired was my sister Hope, although Faith had her share of gentleman admirers." June patted her hair. "I'd give my Aunt Thalia's prize setting hen for a hot bath and clean clothes before I meet Eli."

Sam jumped up and down. "Is that him?"

Flattening her nose against the pane, June squinted. "I don't think so—" Disappointment flooded her. The short, portly man standing at the railing looked nothing like Eli's description. Did Eli neglect to mention his true age? His letters said that he was twenty-three, but the man standing at the side of the railing, his gaze eagerly skimming debarking passengers, looked older than her papa had been.

Sam pressed closer. "Oh dear. He's a bit older than I 'spected."

"Yes . . . he is—a bit." A good twenty years older, but it wasn't the age that mattered so much. What mattered was the trickery. She didn't approve of trickery— not in any form. Eli was an old man!

She clamped her eyes shut, then quickly reopened them. The man on the dock was still there. Closing her eyes again, she silently prayed. *Please, please, please don't let that be Eli.*

Again opening her eyes, she sighed. Well, perhaps Eli thought himself young. What did Aunt Thalia say? Age was a state of mind; if you didn't mind, it didn't matter. But then, Aunt Thalia wasn't marrying Eli!

"You say he's an assistant pastor?"

"Yes, to Isaac Inman, the evangelist."

Mustering a stiff upper lip, she gathered her belongings and prepared to meet Eli Messenger.

Sam trailed behind as June descended the gangplank. June dreaded parting company with the young cockney girl. Sam had been a comfort during the seven-day voyage, and June had grown very fond of her. She hoped they would see each other from time to time.

"I'll miss our teatime talks," Sam confided as she hurried to keep up.

"As will I." June smiled. "Once you're settled, perhaps you can attend services one evening. You can go with Eli and me. You'll be our guest."

"Oh, I'd not be knowing lots about godly men. Met more of the other kind, I have. But Auntie's written of Mr. Inman's Evangelistic Crusade and the wonderful work he's doin'."

June was awash with pride. "Eli is proud to be working with Reverend Inman. He raves about the man's dedication."

"Well, I'll not be in church often. Me mum says me old auntie is a good woman but a very sick one. I suspect I'll have me work cut out, taking care of orphaned tykes. There'll be no time for churchin'."

"There's always time for churching, Sam."

June returned Eli's smile as she stepped off the gangplank. He had kind eyes—dare she hope he had a youngish heart, too? The man extended his hand with a warm smile. "June Kallahan?"

Nodding, June switched her valise to the opposite hand and accepted his outstretched hand. "Eli Messenger?"

The man appeared momentarily abashed before breaking into hearty laughter. "Oh, my, no! I'm Isaac—Isaac Inman, Eli's employer. But thank you, young lady! You've certainly brightened my day!" He pumped her hand vigorously.

Relief flooded June. "You're not Eli! That's wonderful!" She was instantly ashamed. Her cheeks burned, but Reverend Inman just laughed harder.

"Oh—no, I didn't mean 'wonderful you weren't Eli'; I only meant—" Realizing she didn't know *what* she meant, much less what she was saying, she simply returned his smile. "How nice to meet you, Reverend Inman. Eli speaks highly of you in his letters." Drawing Sam to her side, June introduced her. "Reverend Inman, I'd like for you to meet Sam—Samantha Harris."

Reverend Inman grasped Sam's hand in a friendly grip. "I didn't expect to find two lovely creatures coming off that boat."

"Sam and I met on the voyage." June anxiously searched the crowd. "Where is Eli?"

Reverend Inman's features sobered. "Eli has taken ill. He's asked that I escort you to your quarters."

June frowned. "Ill?"

Taking her arm, Reverend Inman turned her toward a long row of waiting carriages. Departing passengers milled about, carrying heavy baggage. "Nothing serious," he assured her. "He's been afield most of the week, and the weather's taken a nasty turn. Seems he's caught a bit of a chill. He thought it best that I come to meet you." Reverend Inman reached for the women's valises. "May I take you somewhere, Miss Harris?"

Sam searched the rows of waiting wagons. "Thank you ever so much, but me auntie said she'd send a driver. . . ." She broke into a grin. "Ow, there 'e is now!" A weathered buckboard with *Angeline's Orphanage* spelled out in large, colorful letters was parked at the back of the row. A white-haired Indian man stood beside the wagon, waiting.

"Are you Angeline's niece?" Reverend Inman asked, surprised.

Sam brightened. "You know me old auntie?"

"Know of her," Reverend Inman said. "Fine woman doing a good job with the children. I understand she's not feeling well."

"No, sir, that's why I'm here. Goin' to 'elp her, I am."

Giving June a hug, Sam reached for her battered valise, her youthful face radiant with excitement. "Promise you'll come see me? And soon!"

Hugging back, June promised. "The orphanage is located where?"

"On the outskirts of town—not far from the crusade grounds. Me auntie says every man, woman, and child in Seattle 'as heard of Angeline's Orphanage."

The two women shared a final brief, warm embrace.

"I'll be keepin' you in me prayers, June Kallahan," Sam whispered.

"As I'll keep you in mine," June promised.

Sam walked to the waiting wagon, and Reverend Inman helped June into the carriage, then took his place behind the reins. As the buggy pulled away, June glanced over her shoulder for a final glimpse of Sam. The elderly driver was loading her valise into the buckboard. Scared and filled with apprehension, she turned back to face the road. Homesickness nearly felled her.

Look on the bright side, June! Soon she would be married, taking care of her new husband.

Tomorrow she wouldn't miss her sisters so much.

Tomorrow she wouldn't listen so intently for the sound of Sam's lyrical cockney accent.

Tomorrow God would remove all her fears.

The pungent air reeked of the vast forests of Douglas firs and red cedars. The smell of wet vegetation stung her nose. The rain had slowed to a light drizzle.

"Oh, my! Just look at those mountains! Aren't they spectacular!" She'd seen pictures of mountains but had never hoped to actually see one.

Reverend Inman clucked, urging the horse through a muddy pothole. "To the east we have the Cascades. To the west, the Olympics. They are quite magnificent, some of God's finest work."

From the moment June had accepted Eli's proposal, she read every book she could get her hands on concerning Seattle. She learned the town was located on a hilly isthmus on Puget Sound. Seattle served primarily as a lumber town and was noted for its abundant natural resources of water, timber, and fish.

"Have you been here long?"

"Seattle is my home. I left for a while, but when my wife passed on, I returned." His eyes grew distant. "The area is fertile for harvest."

The clouds lowered, and a cold wind blew off the inlets as the buggy traveled deeper inland. June burrowed into her cloak, wishing she'd worn something heavier. The worsening weather made it impossible to talk. Instead she watched the road, praying God would safely deliver them from the inclement weather.

It was some time before Reverend Inman finally drew the horse to a halt. June's breath caught at the sight below. A tent, the size of which June had never before witnessed, spread out like a vast city before them. Men, dressed in yellow oil-cloth slickers, wrestled with heavy ropes and cables. The heavens suddenly opened, and the drizzle turned into a deluge. Lightning forked, and the mountains reverberated with the mighty sound of thunder.

June gripped the side of the wagon as Reverend Inman urged the team down the slippery incline. Aunt Thalia's warning rang in her ears. *You're making a mistake, young lady!*

The wagon finally rolled to a stop in front of an unusual-looking octagon-shaped dwelling. June stared at the odd-shaped cinder-block building, thinking it looked very out of place among the ocean of canvas. Sitting low to the ground, the earth-tone complex zigzagged in varying directions, covering at least a half acre of ground. The land surrounding the house unit was barren, with not one blade of grass. In the summer, colorful marigolds and asters might relieve the naked landscape, but today the rain only made it look more bleak.

"We're here," Reverend Inman announced. "Home—for now."

June looked about, fighting another wave of homesickness. The immense revival tent flapped like a giant, awkward bird, two hundred yards to the right of the complex. Home. The connotation sounded peculiar to her, almost frightening.

Climbing out of the buckboard, Reverend Inman extended his hand. "Hurry now, let's get you inside, where it's dry!"

June gathered her damp skirt and stepped down. Thankful to be on solid ground again, she hurried behind Reverend Inman into the shelter of her strange-looking new home. Shivering, she trailed the minister through the corridor and emerged in a brightly lit parlor where a coal stove burned in the middle of the octagon-shaped room.

Reverend Inman shrugged out of his

wet coat, then reached for a small bell and rang it. "I'll have Ettie bring tea."

Momentarily a tiny woman appeared, wearing a flannel nightgown and wrapper. Salt-and-pepper strands peeked from beneath the nightcap framing her weathered face and friendly blue eyes. As Papa would say, she couldn't weigh eighty pounds soaking wet. "You rang, Reverend?"

Reverend Inman smiled with weary gratitude. "I know it's late, but Miss Kallahan and I could use a cup of tea, Ettie. Do you mind?"

"Mind? Of course I don't mind, Reverend. I've been worried about you." She tsked. "Not a fit night for man or beast." She crossed the room, snagging a crocheted throw from a wing chair beside the fire. "You must be Eli's intended."

June nodded, trying to still her chattering teeth. "Yes, ma'am."

"Ettie keeps my house and cooks my meals," Reverend Inman explained. He viewed the wiry woman with open affection. "But, of course, she's much more than a housekeeper. I couldn't manage without her."

"And I couldn't do without you, Reverend. Here now, we need to get you out of those wet clothes. Rain, rain, and more rain," Ettie clucked. "My old bones can't take much more." Pointing to a door on the right, she ordered June, "Go on, now. I'll bring your things in to you. When you've changed, I'll have tea waiting. Reverend, take off those wet shoes." Scurrying purposefully across the floor, she bent down and stoked the fire. Sparks flew up the stovepipe as the embers caught and the flames grew.

June did as she was told, returning a short time later dressed in a dry pewter-colored wool. The smell of fresh-baked bread drew her to the small table Ettie had set. A heaping plate of scones, blackberry jelly, and a bowl of rich yellow butter surrounded a colorful clay pot of steeping tea. June realized she hadn't eaten since breakfast—a meager fare of tea with toast and butter.

"Come. Sit," Ettie ordered.

Reverend Inman appeared through a second doorway. June wondered how many rooms the quaint-looking building had. "Ahh, Ettie, my dear. Hot scones on a rainy night. How did you know that's exactly what I prayed for on the way home?"

Ettie winked at June. "You've prayed the same prayer for the thirty years I've known you, Reverend. By now, the Lord knows it by heart."

Reverend Inman chuckled, holding his hands to the crackling stove.

Ettie poured cups of steaming tea, adding a generous dollop of cream to the reverend's cup. June listened to the affectionate banter between Ettie and the reverend, deciding she was going to like the friendly housekeeper and the gentle evangelist.

Heavy rain pelted the windowpanes as they drank tea and buttered the hot scones. The room was cozy, with an overstuffed sofa, wing chairs, and wool rugs on the pine floors. Reverend Inman's private quarters, June surmised. A long row of bookshelves on the east wall contained books concerning the ministries of Dwight L. Moody and other prominent evangelists of the time. June thought of how eager Papa would have been to read works about these great men. He'd spoken often of Moody and chorister Ira Sankey. The two men traveled the country, preaching to huge crowds and converting thousands to Christianity.

Ettie fussed around the warm room, setting damp shoes on the brick hearth and draping wet coats over a line strung behind the stove. The room smelled of baked bread and steamed wool.

"Will you be needing anything else, Reverend?"

"No, thank you, Ettie. Is Eli awake?"

"Yes, sir. Parker is with him."

"Parker?" The reverend lifted his cup thoughtfully. "Terrible night for visiting."

"Yes, sir. Terrible. But you know how Parker feels about Eli. He refuses to leave his side."

"Yes, yes. He and Eli are good friends."

"That they are, close as bark on a tree. I'll be taking them both tea and scones now."

"You do that, Ettie. Tell Eli we'll be in to say good night shortly."

Ettie left through yet another doorway, which June assumed led to the kitchen. Swallowing the last bite of scone and jelly, she stood up, anxious to meet her intended husband. The trip had been long, and her curiosity was blooming. Who was this man she was about to marry? Was he as kind and gentle as Reverend Inman? Was there anything she could do to hasten his recovery?

Wiping his mouth on a white napkin, Reverend Inman smiled. "I see you're anxious to meet your fiancé."

June smoothed the folds of her skirt, hoping her excitement didn't show. "Yes, sir, I am most anxious to meet Eli."

"Then we must delay no longer." Pushing back from the table, the reverend got slowly to his feet. "Follow me."

June accompanied him through a fourth doorway leading down a long, winding hallway. They passed many closed doors before finally stopping. Rapping softly, the reverend called, "Eli? Do you feel up to visitors?"

Momentarily the door opened, and June shrank back when a man so tall, with shoulders so broad she suddenly felt breathless, blocked their way.

His eyes—incredibly blue eyes—looked past her and fixed on the reverend. He nodded. "Isaac."

Reverend Inman met the man's steady gaze. "I know it's late, but Eli's bride has arrived. Does he feel up to a brief visit?"

The man turned and spoke quietly. June couldn't make out his words. In the background, a weak male voice answered.

Stepping aside, the man ushered them into the room. June walked past him, aware of the faint smell of soap and water. The red-and-black flannel shirt and dark trousers he wore were neatly pressed.

Moving to the bedside, Reverend Inman adjusted the wick on the lamp higher. Shadows danced off the walls as rain pelted the windowpane.

A figure on the bed stirred. "Is that you, Reverend?"

"I've collected your bride safely, Eli."

"Thank you, Brother Isaac. Bring her closer to the light," Eli murmured.

June was troubled by the tremor in his voice. He sounded so very weak. What had the reverend said? Eli had taken ill suddenly? He had caught a chill—well, a chill could take the starch right out of a body. If Eli would permit her, first thing tomorrow morning she would concoct Aunt

Thalia's poultice, made from garlic, honey, and herbs. Very unpleasant to smell but guaranteed to cure whatever ailed a person.

Reverend Inman reached for June's hand and drew her closer to the light. Smiling, she focused on the man who was soon to be her husband. Illness shadowed his lean face. Hazel eyes—much too bright—searched the shadows for her. His boyish features were flushed red, and an inadequate reddish growth that passed for a beard covered his youthful chin. A line of angry sores dotted his bottom lip from the high fever.

Groping for her hand, he said softly, "Hello, June."

June squeezed his fingers, hot to the touch. "Hello, Eli. I'm sorry to hear you're sick. Is there anything I can do to make you more comfortable?"

He shook his head, closing his eyes. "No . . . no, they're taking very good care of me. I'm sorry I wasn't able to meet you. I trust the voyage from San Francisco was uneventful?"

"Yes, quite uneventful—with the exception that I met—" June stepped back as

Eli dissolved in a fit of coughing. The attack was so violent, so all-consuming, that she immediately grew concerned. Reaching for the pitcher on the bedside table, she steadied her hand and poured a glass of water. "Perhaps some water . . ."

The man with the broad shoulders suddenly blocked her efforts. She glanced up to meet his stern look. "Water only makes it worse."

She immediately set the glass down. "I'm sorry."

"This is my friend Parker. Parker Sentell," Eli whispered. "Parker, my intended bride, June Kallahan. She's come all the way from Michigan—" Another round of coughing interrupted the introductions.

June lifted her eyes to meet Parker Sentell's. For a moment their gaze held. Shivers raced down June's spine, and she suddenly felt chilled. He was scrutinizing her—looking her over closely, and she detected resentment in his stormy blue eyes. An awkward moment passed before he briefly inclined his head, silently acknowledging the introduction. A man of few

words, June decided. Instinct told her that
Parker Sentell was trouble.

She wondered how two complete oppo-
sites could form such a close friendship,
yet Eli had written that the bond between
Parker and himself was as strong as that
of brothers.

Parker stationed himself at the doorway,
crossing his arms over his massive chest.
The width of his biceps was as impressive
as the breadth of his shoulders.

He fixed his cool eyes on her.

When the coughing refused to abate,
Reverend Inman gently eased June toward
the doorway. "We'll return in the morning
when you're feeling stronger."

"Thank you . . . Reverend." Eli feebly
lifted an imploring hand to June. "I'm
sorry. . . . Perhaps tomorrow . . ."

"Of course. Tomorrow. I'll come and sit
with you—all day if you'd like."

Nodding, Eli doubled up in another
coughing spasm.

As June slipped past Parker Sentell,
their eyes met again. She resisted the
urge to assure him that nothing would
change for him once she and Eli married.
She would have many friends, as Eli

would. Parker needn't feel threatened by her presence.

But he did. She could see it in the cool depth of his eyes.

Accusation? Animosity? She wasn't sure what was mirrored in his eyes. Nor was she sure why, but the implication was clear: She was an intruder.

Brushing past him, she made a mental note to ask Reverend Inman why this man, this powerful-looking man who was Eli's best friend, was so hostile.

She glanced over her shoulder and shivered at the sight of his intimidating stature. Then again, maybe she didn't want to know.

The reverend retraced their steps through the corridor, and he showed her to her room. The cubicle was adequate but sparse. Octagon-shaped, the small space held a single bed, a washstand, a simple clothespress, and a stove. Wind whistled around the cracks in the walls.

She shivered, spying her valise sitting on the bed.

"Breakfast is at seven."

"Thank you, Reverend." Saying good night, she closed the door and leaned against it as the long day closed in on her. Rain battered the windowpane with unrelenting velocity. What a week this had been. The long trip from Cold Water, Eli's unexpected illness. She sank to the side of the bed, trying to organize her thoughts. Tomorrow she would sit with Eli, and they could talk. They would tell one another all about themselves, and she would get to know her soon-to-be husband. The same intuition that told her Parker Sentell was trouble also told her she was going to like Eli Messenger. He seemed a gentle soul, and he had been most polite, even as bad as he felt.

Yawning, she slipped off the bed and rummaged through her valise for pen, ink, and writing paper. She wanted to share this first exciting day in Seattle with Aunt Thalia.

Dear Auntie,

I am so weary I can hardly keep my eyes open, but I wanted to inform you I have arrived in Seattle without incident. The Lord protected my way, and I made a new friend, Samantha Harris. Sam is here in Seattle to assist her ailing aunt, who runs a small orphanage not far from the crusade grounds. I hope to visit there one day soon.

A few minutes ago Isaac Inman, of the Isaac Inman Evangelistic Crusade, introduced me to my husband-to-be, Eli Messenger. Eli is presently under the weather, but Reverend Inman assures me he will be fit again very soon. Eli's friend, Parker Sentell, was visiting Eli tonight. I understand the two men are good friends. Although I like Eli very much, I personally didn't take to Mr. Sentell. He's certainly one giant of a man, tall, powerfully built, with arms so large they resemble small hams, and eyes . . . eyes, Auntie, so blue they remind me of that robin egg I found one day when I was six. Remember? I brought it to your house for safekeeping.

I sense Mr. Sentell resents my presence here, though why I can't imagine. I will pray that he will be of comfort to Eli during his illness and that in time he will consider me a friend. That said, Auntie, I will say an extraspecial thank-you to the Lord that he has sent me to be a help-

*mate to Eli and not to a man like Mr.
Sentell.*

*I hope this letter finds you well and
happy in the Lord. I miss you, and I
hope I can send money for your passage to Seattle very soon. We will have
a long visit and rejoice in my new life.*

*Your loving niece,
June Kallahan*

Blotting the letter, she folded it, then
laid it aside. Stretching out on the bed,
she listened to the rain pelting the window, wishing she were home in Cold Water, in her warm bed in Aunt Thalia's nor-
mal-shaped attic.

Chapter Two

The rain refused to let up. It came in
heavy sheets, nearly blinding June as she
picked her way along the thin board side-
walk. She was chilled to the bone, and it
was getting dark. Gripping the lantern
tightly in one hand, she bunched her skirt
in the other and cautiously made her way
to the complex. The ground was a quag-
mire.

Sighing, she paused to get her footing,
her attention diverted to the activity taking
place around her. Mules, the biggest
she'd ever seen, pulled wagons heavy-
laden with tents, poles, pews, and equip-
ment necessary to operate the massive

church crusade. Once-lush, green Seattle countryside was mired in thick ruts. Someone had laid boards end to end for a makeshift walkway. Unfortunately, the raw-pine planks didn't always meet in the center. Twice, June snagged the hem of her dress and almost plunged headfirst into the dank mire.

The gloomy weather only added to her growing melancholy. She'd been in Seattle two days, and Eli was still ill—so ill they had yet to have their promised talk.

Each day she made the trek down the hallway to his room, but each day Parker Sentell turned her away, saying, "Eli isn't up to visitors today. You'll have to come back tomorrow." He was polite, but June had the feeling he didn't like her.

Well, who did this Parker Sentell think he was? He protected Eli as if he needed protection from her—*her, his wife-to-be.* She'd spoken to Reverend Inman about the matter, but he only shook his head and suggested she pray that Eli would soon enjoy robust health again. As Eli's intended wife, she had a right to help. She had always been good at nursing people back to health. Parker had no right to exclude her from Eli's illness.

June took her eyes from the board for an instant, and her foot slipped. Hopping around on one foot and waving both arms, she did a desperate dance in an attempt to steady herself and keep from sitting down in the muck. She managed not to fall down. But one foot landed on the board; the other sank up to her ankle in gray slime. Muttering under her breath, she jerked free, but her boot remained buried.

Heaving a huge sigh, she glanced around to see who, if anyone, had witnessed the spectacle. Men whistled and called to their mule teams, but most seemed unaware of her predicament.

With a great sucking sound, she broke the mud's hold and pulled her boot free. She was drenched, chilled to the bone, and feeling more than a little foolish. It would take an hour to scrape the mud off that boot.

She continued down the walk in an uneven gait, wearing one boot and holding the other in the hand that held the lantern.

The saturated planks were icy beneath her stockinged foot.

As she approached her quarters, lightning split the sky. A clap of thunder jarred the ground, and the clouds opened up and poured. She quickly ducked inside the complex, wondering if coming to Washington had been the right thing to do. She thought of Aunt Thalia's parlor in Cold Water. The old house was drafty but always comfortable. It was nothing like the strange-looking complex that was supposed to be her new home.

Scraping mud off her boot, she swallowed against the thick lump forming in her throat. She thought of her sisters; Faith was in Texas, Hope in Kentucky. They might as well have been at the ends of the earth. How long would it be before the sisters were reunited? She didn't want to think of how long. Right now, it felt like an eternity.

Lord, forgive me for fretting over material things like warm parlors and happy talks with my sisters when you've given me a new start.

Taking a deep breath, she brightened. She might be barely seventeen, but she was about to marry a preacher—or almost a preacher. Eli was only an assistant pastor, but he would be a preacher someday. And as a minister's wife, certain things would be expected of her.

She vowed to relinquish her selfish thoughts and endure whatever it took to be a loving wife and devoted helpmate to Eli. A supportive wife, wholeheartedly involved in his ministry. Shivers ran up her back just thinking about it. She, June Kallahan, a preacher's wife. And one day, the mother of Preacher Eli's children. Growing up as a preacher's kid, she had dreamt of marrying a wonderful man like Papa. Now here she was, a mail-order bride to a preacher. God had provided her with her dream.

Dropping the lantern on the tabletop, she shrugged out of the raincoat and hung it up to dry. The long braid she'd so carefully plaited earlier was now plastered to her back. Releasing the buttons on her wet dress, she stepped out of it and draped the wet garment across the back of the chair. She suddenly recalled the letter Parker Sentell had thrust through the partially opened door, stating that it had arrived that morning from Eli's mother. "Read it somewhere dry," he'd said. As if she would sit down in the middle of a downpour and read mail!

June admitted that her thoughts about Parker Sentell weren't exactly charitable, and she had to bite her tongue to remain civil whenever she saw him. If Eli considered Parker a friend, she would like to share that friendship too. But it didn't look as if it would be easy.

Rummaging through her satchel, she located her flannel gown and robe and quickly changed into the warmth of the dry nightclothes. Wrapping her wet hair in a towel, she stifled a sneeze, praying she wasn't coming down with a cold.

She removed the envelope from her dress pocket and sat down on the side of the bed.

Eli filled her thoughts, and she wondered if he thought often of her. What was his impression of her? She considered herself somewhat of a plain soul even if Sam didn't. Even more so, when compared to her sisters, Faith and Hope. She often wondered why Papa hadn't just named her Jane. Plain Jane. But instead

he named her June. June, though a pretty
month, seemed rather uninspired for a
name. Charity—now that would have been
more appropriate. Faith, Hope, and Charity. But Mama had died giving birth to her,
and Papa, in blind grief, hadn't felt very
charitable toward his new infant daughter.
June, he declared. Her name would be
June. So June it was, but charity was
close to June's heart. Helping others gave
her a peace she couldn't explain. It was
an intricate part of her, a part she needed
to fulfill in order to feel whole.

Deep down, it didn't matter that she
was rather ordinary looking and without
any remarkable strengths. The heavenly
Father may not have seen fit to make her
as independent as Faith or as beautiful as
Hope, but he had blessed her with a singing voice. More than one kind soul had
remarked that she had a voice superior to
most, young or old. She didn't think so,
but she hoped the good Lord saw fit to let
her use her talent—however small—in Eli's
ministry.

Slipping her fingertips along the envelope seal, she carefully opened the letter.
Eli's mother had sent the letter all the way

from Ohio for her son's new bride. But
there was more than just a letter enclosed.
Inside the pages was a neatly folded
handkerchief. June admired the pale blue
fine linen, crisply starched and trimmed
with delicate white lace. For a moment
she held the gift close to her heart, inhal-
ing its subtle lavender fragrance.

As nice as the present was, she
couldn't wait to read Mrs. Messenger's
words. She quickly unfolded the pages.

Dearest June,

*I hope you won't mind my taking the
liberty of addressing you by your first
name. When Eli wrote, telling us of his
plans to marry, his father and I were
elated. We wish you and our son great
happiness. Perhaps when you're settled,
we can come and visit you.*

*When Eli wrote last year, informing us
of the accident, we were gravely concerned. Eli explained how a tree had
fallen on him and crushed his leg.
Parker Sentell, Eli's boss and very good
friend, took Eli under his care and se-
cured for him the services of the finest
surgeon to be found in Seattle. After the*

operation and much time spent recuperating, Eli says his limp is only slightly noticeable.

We were very grateful to the Lord and Parker Sentell. And, of course, to Reverend Inman. I'm certain you can imagine our joy when Eli wrote that he had accepted the Lord's call to preach the gospel. It was the answer to our prayers. To have a son in the ministry! And now, to know he has chosen a wife who shares his love for the Lord. Well, it doesn't get any better! Except, of course, when the grandchildren start to arrive.

I hope you like the enclosed wedding gift. It was Eli's paternal great-grandmother's, and was given to me on my wedding day. I want you to have it.

I pray many happy and prosperous years embrace your marriage. We are anxiously waiting to hear from you.

Love,

Ruth and Paul Messenger

June sat for a moment, holding the letter. Ruth Messenger's thoughtfulness already made her feel a welcomed part of the family.

Folding the letter back into the envelope, June placed the handkerchief inside her satchel with the rest of her wedding attire. She would carry it on top of her Bible as soon as Eli was well enough for the ceremony.

Kneeling beside the small cot, she prayed for Eli's health to be restored, for his family, and for their forthcoming marriage.

Slipping beneath the cool sheets, she fell asleep to the sound of rain hammering the roof, content in the belief that morning would bring Eli's first real signs of recovery.

Early the next morning she stepped out of the house, pausing to lift her face to the sun. Sunshine streamed down, and the rays felt gloriously warm! Not only had the rain ceased, but the sky was a brilliant blue—so blue, she thought of Parker Sentell's eyes and frowned.

Deep green forests, towering Douglas

firs, Sitka spruce, and western redwoods soared into the heavens.

Drawing a cleansing breath, she spun around and around, lifting her arms in praise. *Thank you, heavenly Father! A day this beautiful can be nothing but special!*

Hurrying back inside, she quickly covered the distance to Eli's room, thinking she would mention Aunt Thalia's poultice if he weren't greatly improved this morning.

Pausing before his door, she rapped twice, hoping Mr. Sentell had decided to go to work today. He must work—a man with arms the size of fence posts didn't just sit all day.

"Come in."

June couldn't believe her luck when she recognized Eli's voice. She opened the door a crack and peeked in. Eli was propped up in the bed, looking very pale but improved from the first time she saw him. His voice was weak, yet the illness had done nothing to erase the friendly smile now hovering on his full mouth.

"You are looking much better today," June assured him with a warm smile.

"I'm feeling much better," Eli said. "I'm feeling almost human this morning."

His color reminded June of a time Faith was gravely ill with the fever. They'd almost lost her. Brushing the disturbing thought aside, she reminded herself to be thankful Eli had a little color now. June closed the door, then approached the bed to fluff his pillows. "Have you eaten?"

"Ettie brought a tray in earlier. I managed to eat some hot cereal."

"That's a start!" She poured a glass of fresh water and handed him the cup.

He looked up gratefully, his hand trembling as he drank. "Thank you. I'm trying to force myself to eat—I need the strength."

June waited until he drank a few swallows before she leaned over to steady his hand.

"Thank you."

She smiled.

"Did Isaac meet the ship on time?"

"Yes, he was waiting when it docked. Thank you for sending him. It was very thoughtful of you."

Eli dismissed her gratitude. "I'm sorry I couldn't be there to meet you myself."

"I understood. I wish you could have met Sam."

"Sam?"

"Yes, she's here to help her aunt, who runs the orphanage not far from here."

"Oh . . . yes, I've seen the place. Angeline's, isn't it?"

"Yes, Angeline is Sam's aunt."

He took a last sip, then set the cup aside. "I was afraid you were ready to run back to Michigan when you got your first look at me the other night."

"No, not at all! Why would you think that?"

He chuckled softly. "I fear I must make a pitiful sight."

"Don't be silly." Her cheeks grew warm. "You're very handsome. I'm not at all disappointed." She straightened the mussed blankets, then sat down in the straightback chair next to the bed. He obviously was going to need nursing; maybe he would allow her to help. Crossing her hands in her lap, she studied the pattern on the rug on the floor.

The silence stretched. Her mind raced with a million thoughts. Now that he was feeling better and able to get a clear look

at her, was *he* having second notions?
Had he expected someone prettier? Thin-
ner? More outgoing?

No, she reasoned away the insecure
thought. She'd been completely honest
with Eli Messenger when she responded
to his ad. She had enclosed a small tin-
type of herself, so unless he were blind—
which she could clearly see he wasn't—he
would have known she was no raving
beauty. She glanced up to find Eli studying her.

He gave a wan smile. "Penny for your
thoughts."

June blushed. "You wouldn't be getting
your money's worth."

"Oh, I don't know about that. You look
very serious."

If he only knew her wayward thoughts,
she'd die of embarrassment. Thank goodness Eli was an assistant preacher and
not a mind reader.

"Would you like for me to read to you?"
she asked.

"Not now. I'd like to just talk."

"Of course." She shifted in the chair,
crossing and then recrossing her hands.

"You met Parker, didn't you?"

She frowned. "Yes."

With an attempt at another smile, Eli lay back against the pillow. "Is that a frown I see?"

"I'm sorry. It is. Parker doesn't seem to like me."

Eli closed his eyes. "You and Parker aren't getting along?"

"Oh . . . it isn't that." She could hardly tell him that she didn't like his friend. She barely knew Mr. Sentell. She would allow she might be misjudging him. "If you like him, that's all that matters."

Eli lay for a moment, gathering the strength to speak. "When I'm stronger, we'll talk about Parker and what an exceptional friend he has been to me. No man could have any better. Parker's accustomed to working with loggers—I'm afraid he overlooks etiquette when he's around a woman. Too, Parker and the reverend don't see eye to eye on Isaac's tabernacle. When Isaac's around, Parker tends to be difficult to get along with."

Once again silence lapsed between them.

"Well, I don't want to overly tire you. I'll be going along—unless, of course, there's anything you need." June stood up, ready to leave.

Eli opened his eyes. "Resting is the one thing I'm getting very tired of doing."

"I know it must be difficult to be confined to a sickbed. It won't be long before you're up and around again."

"Yes . . . I'll certainly welcome that. But don't go—I want you to stay."

June started to protest, but the sincerity in his hazel eyes touched her.

"We've barely begun to talk. I'll rest for a moment; then we can visit. Please . . . stay."

Moving the chair closer, she sat down again. "Of course, I'll be happy to stay."

She returned his attempted good-natured smile. Was he courting her? She wasn't sure because no one had ever courted her before. But she supposed he could be. After all, they were about to be married. It would be proper enough. She smiled. "Your mother sent me your great-grandmother's lovely handkerchief for the wedding. It was so thoughtful of her."

"That's Mama. . . . Always eager to do something nice for someone." He appeared to doze for a moment.

If she had harbored any lingering doubts about coming west, these past few moments with Eli erased them. It was surely God's plan for her life—a life devoted to Eli Messenger.

"Do you think you could eat again? I could have Ettie fix something light."

Eli shook his head. "No, she'll be bringing lunch soon. Fusses over me like an old mother hen." He lay still for a moment, and June could see his strength fade. "Has Isaac shown you around?"

"No, he's been very busy. It seems he works day and night."

"Yes, he does. He cares so much for his people."

"My, the crusade tent—it's the biggest tent I've ever seen. Why, it's even bigger than the one I saw when Aunt Thalia took us to a circus in Lansing one year."

Eli smiled, and June realized she was babbling. She must go now and let him rest. He obviously wasn't out of the woods. "Not that I'm comparing the revival tent to a circus—but then, you're tired. I really must go," she said, rising.

"No, please . . . I want to talk."

June liked his gentle ways and the way

he made her feel at ease. It was going to be a very good marriage.

Against her better judgment, she took her seat a third time. "Just a little longer."

Eli opened his eyes, and they'd taken on a sudden shine. "I want to tell you about Isaac. He's been preaching over thirty years, traveled the revival circuit, been practically everywhere." He stopped for a moment, then began again. "He was with Jeremiah Lanphier at one time. You've heard of Lanphier? Jeremiah started weekly noon prayer meetings in New York City. Within months there were over six thousand people participating in daily prayer services."

June listened to the warmth in Eli's voice. He loved Reverend Inman deeply. "I don't think I've ever seen that many people in my whole life."

Eli smiled. "In May of that same year, fifty thousand people were converted."

"Praise God."

"The next year, Isaac traveled with a crusade to England."

"My . . . all the way across the ocean?" June couldn't imagine that, yet

Sam had heard of Reverend Inman's ministry.

"All that way. Tragically, his wife of forty years passed away on the voyage back. Katherine had a powerful dream, one she and Isaac shared. A vision, actually."

"A vision?"

"The tabernacle. When Katherine was in New York, she saw the cathedrals of Saint Patrick and Saint John the Divine. Both she and Isaac were deeply moved, but it wasn't until they traveled to England and saw the Lincoln and other cathedrals that Isaac was truly inspired."

"Inspired to do what?"

"To build his own church. But not just a church. A tabernacle, a magnificent place to worship and glorify God," Eli said, with great pride reflected in his voice. "Katherine shared that dream. Her dying words were, 'Build our cathedral, Isaac. Build it for the glory of God.' " Eli's eyes closed momentarily, then opened.

"A cathedral? Here? In the middle of the woods?"

June's question seemed to renew his strength. "Here—on the land Isaac and Katherine purchased a few years back.

Seattle is growing, June. The growth is precisely what's needed to accommodate the large congregation Isaac is acquiring."

"The only kind of church I've ever attended was one room—"

"Visualize it, June! See it—dream about it. Isaac, like King David in the Old Testament, desires to build a splendid tabernacle to the Lord, using only the best because the Lord deserves the best. Isaac and Katherine wanted to build something that would attest to the greatness of God."

"Yes, I *can* see it," she murmured.

"Every detail. An elegant handcrafted altar, made from the finest mahogany. Scarlet fabric cushioning the multitude of pews. A choir stall. Brass pillars. Stained-glass windows, each telling in mosaic beauty the story of Christianity. Magnificent materials and detailed workmanship, right down to candlesticks made of pure gold. Nothing but the best for the Lord."

June was spellbound. She'd never heard of such grandeur, let alone seen anything as splendid as the church Eli described. It was a wonderful dream—a glorious tribute to God's presence. "When does Reverend Inman plan to build this church?"

"Tabernacle. And we'll build it as soon as there are sufficient funds. If God continues to bless as he has, it will be within the year."

"You must be very excited to be a part of the dream," June said.

"Yes . . . yes. I want to give God my best. Once the people see the magnificent building, it is our belief that they will experience God's grace as well."

Eli was clearly exhausted. Rising from her chair, June straightened his pillows. "I've worn you out. Thank you for sharing your dream." When he voiced a weak protest, she said softly, "I'll come back first thing in the morning."

"I'll look forward to it." Eli grasped her hand warmly. "Thank you for spending this time with me. It's been one of the nicest mornings of my life."

"Thank you, Eli. Sleep well. I'll visit again tomorrow." She touched her fingers to her lips, then lay them across his forehead. It felt hot to her touch. "Sweet dreams."

Chapter Three

Eli was recovering, and they could be
married soon. June wanted to get on with
the Lord's work with Eli at her side. After
their talk yesterday she, too, could visualize the tabernacle. What a tribute to God's
glory! She wanted to be part of building
the monument, part of the dream. In a
small way she would be building a tribute
to Papa for all the years he'd spent
preaching the gospel. Papa's name
wouldn't be on the tabernacle, but in her
heart she would know that the monument
represented a part of him.

It would take a good while for Eli to
regain his strength, even longer to collect

sufficient funds to build the tabernacle. He had seemed so much weaker after their talk than when she entered his room. She would keep her visit brief today.

She brushed her hair until it crackled, then tied it back with a pink ribbon. Papa would have been proud to have Eli for a son-in-law. Sitting for a moment, she stared at her mirrored reflection. Eli Messenger was everything Ruth had written about her son, and more.

June's plainness had no effect on him.

Her heart swelled when she realized that Eli was one of a rare breed of men who looked beyond the exterior and sought a person's inner beauty. "Thank you, God, for giving me such a perceptive husband. And a handsome one, too. You're far too good to me."

She pinched her cheeks for a little color. She must write both sisters immediately after her visit with Eli this morning. If Eli felt up to it, they could both write. Faith and Hope would be happy to hear from their new brother-in-law.

Moments later she walked down the corridor carrying a basket of oranges. Ettie had purchased the fruit the day before, saying they were Eli's favorite. Humming under her breath, she smiled when she saw Reverend Inman walking toward her. It was his custom to visit Eli early before he started the busy day.

"Good morning, Reverend—"

Isaac took her by the arm and turned her around, urging her back down the corridor. Puzzled, she followed, wondering why he was acting so strangely.

Steering her back into her room, he closed the door.

"Reverend Inman—?"

Drawing a deep breath, he ran his hands over his ashen features. June's heart tripped as she sank to the side of the bed. The reverend looked as if he'd just seen a ghost! Something must have happened with the crusade.

Edging forward, her eyes anxiously searched his. "What's wrong, Reverend?"

"It's—" his voice cracked, then steadied—"It's . . . Eli."

"Eli?" She felt the blood drain from her face. "Has he had a setback? He seemed to be feeling much better when I left yesterday—"

Shaking his head, the reverend took her hand. Tears filled his eyes, and he said softly, "There's no easy way to tell you, June. Eli is gone."

"Gone?" June's mind whirled. "Gone where?" Her heart sank. Oh, dear Lord. Gone. Eli had started thinking about the marriage and her plainness and decided to go back to Ohio—

"But he was so weak—he wasn't able to travel—"

Reverend Inman bowed his head, his voice barely a whisper. "Gone." The silence was unbearable. A million images raced through June's mind. Eli gone? Even if he were feeling better, where could he have gone in the middle of the night?

"When . . . when did he leave?" June struggled to maintain her composure. The news was devastating. How could she have been so taken with Eli—felt so good about him and the marriage—and been so wrong?

"A few moments ago," the reverend said softly. "I'm sorry. . . . It was so unexpected. . . . There was no time. . . ."

June's anger swelled as the implication

of Eli's actions hit her. "You don't need to apologize for Eli. If he didn't have the decency to say good-bye—"

"June." The solemnity in the reverend's voice stopped her. "My dear—" he bent forward, squeezing her hand gently—"I'm so sorry—you misunderstand. Eli's gone home . . . to be with the Lord."

For a moment June couldn't comprehend the enormity of what he was saying.

"I am so very, very sorry." The reverend's face crumpled, and he began to weep. "Eli was like a son to me."

Sliding off the bed, June held him as his sobs filled the room. She had never witnessed such pain. The exhibition tore at her heart.

"We don't understand God's ways," Reverend Inman said brokenly, "but we have to believe there's a reason for everything that happens." His features constricted. "God forgive me, I can't imagine what it would be . . . taking Eli when. . . ." Words failed him.

"Eli . . . gone," June whispered as the realization sank in. Eli was dead. "But why? Why?" she cried. "Yesterday he was feeling . . . I prayed . . . prayed so hard for him."

Reverend Inman fumbled in his pocket for his handkerchief. "I have no explanation. . . . He seemed to be improving. Toward dawn his fever came up again, and he was having trouble catching his breath. He rang for Ettie. She came for me, and . . . an hour later he slipped away."

June bit her lip, shaking her head. Tears welled to her eyes. Eli gone? Why did God bring her to this faraway place to marry such a wonderful man, only to call him home before their life together ever started? June experienced something foreign to her. Doubt. Why would God do something so unfair to Eli? His life had barely begun. . . . There was so much he wanted to do to help build the reverend's tabernacle.

"Oh, Reverend Inman." She held the older man as he broke down again. What a grievous loss this kind man must feel. She barely knew Eli, and she was overcome by news of his death. What must the reverend be feeling?

When the wave of sorrow receded, he

got unsteadily to his feet. Blowing his nose, he shook his head, trying to regain his composure. "His family must be told."

June thought of Ruth Messenger's glowing letter, Eli's great-grandmother's lovely handkerchief—the family would be heartbroken.

She patted Reverend Inman's shoulder, fortifying herself for the terrible task that lay ahead. "I will tell Eli's parents of his death and make arrangements for his burial."

"I can't allow you to do that, June. You've only just arrived."

"Please, Reverend Inman. I need to do this. I know Eli and I weren't married, but in a way I feel as if we were. Let me do this, for both you and Eli."

"Parker—"

She swallowed, steeling herself for the most onerous task of all. "I will inform Parker." It wouldn't be the easiest thing she'd ever done, but then, it wouldn't be the hardest.

Coming to grips with the knowledge that she was a widow before she was ever a bride was the hardest thing.

My dear Mr. and Mrs. Messenger:

It is with the deepest regret that I write this letter. Your beloved son, Eli, passed away early this morning. He had been ill for nearly a week but expected to fully recover. We tended him and prayed for his healing; still, God saw best to call him home.

Eli was everything you said and more. And though we had yet to marry, I shall forever feel the loss of this wonderful man I was given the pleasure of knowing for even a brief time. I pray God will give you and your family abundant comfort in your time of need.

You will remain in my thoughts and prayers, as Eli will always hold a special place in my heart.

Yours in Christian love,
June Kallahan

Before sealing the envelope, June gently tucked the handkerchief inside.

Her bravado slipped, and she really wept for the first time, still unable to believe that Eli was dead.

Later that morning June sat on a horse,
looking down on Pine Ridge Logging
Camp. This was Parker Sentell's world.
Teams of oxen were skidding logs from
the cutting area to the landing. June could
hear the sound of axes biting into trees
and the occasional shout of "Timber!" in
the distance.

Parker's camp appeared to be hacked
out of the dense woods, and one of the
bigger, better managed outfits. Beyond
the string of bunkhouses and the cook-
shack/dining room were the office/living
quarters for the bosses and a large barn
containing oxen and what looked to be a
milk cow. June spotted the river. Logs
were stacked high on miles of rollways
along the banks, where they awaited the
spring log drive to the mills.

Reverend Inman had told her that
Parker ran Pine Ridge and oversaw four
smaller camps. Men respected him, if not
for his size and position, then because
they knew they were dependent upon him
for work. Loggers came and went. If a
man didn't work for Sentell now, he eventually could.

June couldn't imagine women in camp.

Not many would subject families to such primitive living conditions.

Nudging the horse's flanks, she rode down the small incline into camp and stopped in front of the office.

"A little far from home, aren't you, Miss Kallahan?"

Her horse shied at the sound of Parker's voice as he reached out and grasped hold of the bridle. She was met with distant blue eyes.

Her arrival attracted a small crowd. Shantyboys stopped what they were doing to stare at the newcomer. June didn't want to break the news of Eli's death to Parker in front of others. Eli's sudden passing would be hard enough for Parker to accept. "May I speak to you in private, Mr. Sentell?"

His eyes narrowed with impatience. "Concerning what?"

"In private, please." She started to dismount, surprised when she felt his hands lifting her slight weight off the saddle.

"What's this about? Is Eli worse?" Concern tinged his voice.

She glanced around, spotting the cookshack. "Can we talk in private there?"

He directed her toward a long, low building with smoke curling from the chimney. It was warm inside, and in spite of the spartan interior, the pleasant aroma of coffee mingled with fried potatoes, sowbelly, flapjacks, and molasses syrup.

"Coffee?"

"No, thank you."

Long tables flanked by plain benches stretched the length of the room. At one end a thin man with a knitted cap stood in front of the big iron cooking range and stirred a huge pot.

Motioning for her to take a seat at the far end of a bench, Parker took the seat opposite her.

"What's this all about?"

June folded her hands, then took a deep breath. "It's Eli."

"What's wrong? He was better yesterday."

"I know. . . . I'm sorry, Parker." There was no easy way to tell him. She was feeling what Reverend Inman must have felt when he broke the news to her. That seemed like days ago. Better to get it out, then try to offer him comfort and prayer. "Eli passed away early this morning."

Color drained from his face, and compassion flooded her. He and Eli had been close, yet, because he was a man, he couldn't cry; he would be expected to buck up.

"We'd hoped . . ."

Parker's fist slammed against the table, and he got up.

June patiently waited for the initial storm to pass. Papa's emotions had flared easily, but he got over it just as quickly.

"No," Parker said tightly. He strode to the window, rubbing his clean-shaven chin. Gripping the top of the window frame, he stared at the activity going on outside.

June wished she had the proper words of condolence. Eli's death was so sudden, so unexpected, that she could barely grasp it herself. "I'm sorry. I know you had a great deal of respect for Eli—"

Parker turned. "Why?"

"Why?"

"Why did God take him?"

June sighed. She had expected sadness, yes, even disbelief, but not anger. She could never understand why the bereaved were often so quick to blame God

for what appeared to be senseless tragedy. "Parker, are you a Christian?"

His shoulders filled the breadth of the
small window. For a long time he didn't
answer. Finally he said in a low voice, "I
accept Jesus as my Savior, if that's what
you're asking."

"Then how can you blame him for Eli's
death?"

A muscle in his jaw firmed. "Eli's death
doesn't make any sense. I get mad, Miss
Kallahan, when a man is taken in his
prime for no reason at all."

"Eli's passing doesn't make sense to
us, but it does to God. He always
knows—has always known—what is right,
what is best."

His expression closed. "There's no purpose for Eli's death. It shouldn't have happened."

She chose not to get into a discussion
of whether God knew what he was doing.
There was no point in such a discussion.
God was always right. Parker must know
that. Grief was speaking.

"We may not always agree with God,
but he doesn't make mistakes."

Parker turned from the window. "Isaac is responsible for this."

"Isaac? Reverend Inman?" What could he possibly have to do with Eli's death?

"The 'dream,' the tabernacle!" Parker snapped. "Eli was consumed with the thought—spoke of nothing else but his dream of building Isaac's tabernacle, some great shrine to draw people." Bitterness tinged his voice. "Perhaps, as I've argued all along, it wasn't *God's* plan but Isaac's."

"Of course you're at liberty to believe whatever you like."

Parker paced back and forth, his hands gripped at his sides. He talked more to himself than to her. "God's not interested in buildings or any of the other trappings that people say they need to glorify him. This is for Isaac's glory."

How could this man call himself Eli's friend and have such thoughts? It was for God's glory, not Reverend Inman's, that Eli dreamed of the tabernacle.

"I understand you're overwrought, Mr. Sentell." June stood up so she didn't have to look up quite so far to talk to him. "I understand your grief and share it—"

"How can you share my grief? You barely knew Eli."

That was true. But she'd known him long enough to know he would be appalled at his friend's reaction. "I knew him long enough to know that I could have loved him deeply." For Eli's sake she couldn't let the issue of the tabernacle go unchallenged. "Reverend Inman's dream is to provide a place of worship, a place like no other. Eli shared that dream, worked hard to fulfill it. God deserves our finest."

"Don't give me that. God doesn't require monuments."

"Of course, that's true—"

"People around here aren't used to grand buildings, Miss Kallahan. Life is hard. I don't know about Cold Water, Michigan, but life in Seattle, Washington, is hard. Most of the community works in one of the logging camps. And life in a logging camp is hard. It's all a man can do to hold it together. They work six days a week and don't see wives and families until spring breakup or the end of the log drives."

He gestured toward the door. "Most

come from distant parts and have few contacts with the fairer sex because of the isolation. That can make a man testy, Miss Kallahan. Real testy. The men earn between twenty-five and thirty dollars a month, plus board. They live in drafty cabins built from lumber they cut themselves. We're common folk, Miss Kallahan. We believe in God, and we can worship him in a tar-paper shack if necessary. I never doubted Eli's sincerity, but we don't need a tabernacle to make us feel better about ourselves."

June could hardly disagree. She believed in all the things he'd listed, but there was nothing wrong with building a monument to God. Reverend Inman was a man pure of heart. His tabernacle would be a glory to God, not a hindrance to his Word.

"The tabernacle will be a place set apart, a place where people from far and wide will come to worship."

"A place Isaac builds in his wife's memory—worse yet, as a tribute to himself."

"The building is a tribute to God," she retorted, irritated that he would have such thoughts. He simply didn't understand what Reverend Inman was trying to do. "It's saying we love God enough to build a special place in which to worship him."

"The Bible says we're to worship God in spirit and in truth. Nothing is said about a fine building being a requirement."

"I cannot believe you are saying this— wasn't Eli your friend?"

Parker leaned toward her, spearing her with a sharpened gaze. "Eli's gone. The matter no longer concerns you. You're entitled to your opinion, but you're not entitled to mine. Go home, Miss Kallahan. There's nothing here for you any longer."

Until this very moment she hadn't considered what she would do, but now the answer was abundantly clear. "I plan to stay on and continue Eli's work with Reverend Inman."

Bracing his broad hands on the tabletop, he leaned in closer, his voice low. "Go home."

"I'm staying on." June raised her chin a notch and met his fixed gaze. "I'm going to help the reverend raise the funds to build the tabernacle."

Parker looked at her for a long moment, then turned on his heel and strode out of the building, anger clear in the set of his shoulders. The door slammed behind him, rattling dishes.

Sinking to the bench, June released the pent-up breath she hadn't realized she'd been holding. No one needed to tell her the battle lines were drawn. She would rather have Parker Sentell as a friend than a foe, but even his boorish and decidedly rude manner wouldn't stop her.

God had a purpose for her in Seattle. She'd thought it was to marry Eli and help in his ministry. With Eli gone, she must wait and pray for God to reveal his will. Meanwhile, she would assist Reverend Inman. . . .

Her eyes followed Parker Sentell's angry gait, watching him march toward his office.

. . . And avoid Parker Sentell whenever possible.

Eli was dead. Parker's hands shook as he jerked the knot on his tie free and started again.

In a few hours he would bury his best friend. Grief washed over him, so forceful he nearly dropped to his knees. *Why, God?* his soul cried. *Why Eli?* Parker bit back bitter tears. *Why would you take Eli when he worked so diligently for your kingdom?* Parker might not have approved of Eli's goals, but he loved Eli like a brother.

Taking a deep breath, he forced his thoughts to Eli's bride. June Kallahan. What should he do with her? She wasn't his responsibility, yet Eli would expect him to look after her welfare. He swallowed around the tight lump crowding his throat. Blast Eli for being so idealistic! What man assumed he could just send for a bride and eternal bliss would reign? Didn't he know that wasn't the way love worked? A man and a woman needed feelings— strong feelings you couldn't buy as a result of an ad in a journal. What was Eli thinking? He jerked the tie and started over.

His angry thoughts tumbled over each other. *Working himself to death to serve Isaac Inman—going from dawn to dusk in an effort to build that temple that was Isaac's obsession, not necessarily God's will.*

Parker had never approved of the tabernacle, and he never would. And he didn't approve of Isaac Inman. Some said he was wrong about Isaac, that the evangelist was a true man of God. But Parker saw little indication of that. He saw a man consumed by his own wants. As far as he was concerned, Isaac should have stuck to his traveling crusade and should not be trying to force his dreams of grandeur off on Seattle. Folks here didn't need his kind. He'd made that clear to Eli, but Eli never argued. He just smiled that good-natured smile and asked Parker to pray about it. Parker had given up trying to talk sense into him. Eli's mind was bent on helping build that temple, and nothing Parker said changed it.

Well, where is endless bliss now, Eli? And what do you expect me to do with the woman you ordered?

The harsh thought faded as the crushing loss closed around him. What would he do without Eli's friendship to brighten the long days? How he would miss his friend's smile and his sense of goodness. The times they'd spent in prayer and fellowship. He blinked, clearing the mositure now clouding his view.

What would God have him to do about Miss Kallahan? She looked as delicate as an orchid, a citified woman, all sweet and helpless.

He frowned at his reflection in the mirror. She wouldn't have lasted more than six months in these wilds—a year at best. And he'd bet she would be gone before the first shovelful of dirt hit Eli's casket.

Somehow the thought made him feel better.

Yes, June Kallahan would return to Michigan or Minnesota or whatever "M" state she was from, and he wouldn't have to worry about her. Out of every tragedy emerges a purpose—isn't that what his mother contended? Who knows? Maybe Eli's death would even cause Isaac to reappraise his objective, and Parker would be rid of two nuisances—June Kallahan and Isaac Inman.

Closing his eyes, he said softly, "The marriage might have worked, Eli, but your new bride seemed a little bossy to me."

The morning of Eli's funeral dawned cool, the sun hidden behind clouds just as death hid Eli's light from the world. How appropriate, June thought, considering the sadness of those who knew and loved the young, aspiring pastor. Everyone June met said how they'd cherished his warmth, his genuine concern, his love of God. Many said that with his passing it was as if a part of them had been taken with him.

For herself, she was determined to dwell on the knowledge that Eli was today with God. His pain was gone, his hope in eternal life realized. She smiled to herself, thinking of the day she would see Eli again and walk with him in that perfect place made for all who belong to God. Keeping her thoughts centered made the day ahead bearable.

She busied herself with preparations for the ceremony. Today, more than ever, she thought about those she loved. Aunt Thalia kept coming to mind, and Papa. What would Papa think of this misadventure? Would he think the building of a tabernacle a worthy cause? She wasn't sure he would. Papa had the soul of a humble man, and any sort of venture that might

be deemed "glorious," as Reverend Inman was wont to describe his vision of
the tabernacle, would immediately be suspect as a prideful idea. But Papa would
look at the motivation behind the desire
for the tabernacle. Was it truly for God's
glory? Then, likely, Papa would approve.
Certainly Eli's motives had been pure.

Today, more than she usually allowed
herself, she missed Faith and Hope. Beautiful Hope, in Kentucky; tomboy Faith, in
Texas. How were each of her sisters far-
ing? It would take so long for letters to
reach her.

Sometimes she worried about whether
her sisters were safe and happy, but then,
the Kallahan girls had always relied on
God to take care of them. She had no
less faith that he would continue to do so.

Quick on the heels of that thought came
the wish that she herself would one day
find the man God intended for her. She
was awash with sadness when she
thought of Eli, lying so still and pale in a
simple pine box in the large crusade tent.
All day long, friends and mourners filed
past, laying floral tributes and simple to-
kens of love at the base of the casket.

Eli no longer occupied his earthly body;
she knew that. Eli sat at the feet of God,
and she was heartened in the knowledge.
As the time for the funeral approached,
the tent began to fill. Eyes reddened,
heads bowed, and voices turned to rever-
ent whispers.

June sat on the front pew beside Reverend Inman and Parker Sentell. When she
glanced at Parker, she saw his jaw working with emotion, but his eyes remained
dry. She smothered the urge to lean closer
and comfort him.

Every seat in the tent was filled by the
time Reverend Inman rose to address the
mourners. As his gaze moved across the
gathering, he conveyed a private message
of comfort to each one. Without looking at
the Bible, he began speaking.

"We are gathered today to pay tribute
to a dear friend. Eli was not just a good
friend, a beloved husband-to-be, a community spiritual leader, a brother in Christ.
Eli was so much more." The reverend's
eyes softened. "To me, he was the son I
never had. To his intended bride, he was

the hope of a shining future. To others, he was a confidant, a safe harbor from life's storms. We will miss him deeply.

"Some will ask, why? Why would a man so young, living his life so purposefully, be called home when his work had barely begun? We do not know why. God's timetable is not our timetable. Shall we wring our hands and weep for understanding, or will we join hands and rejoice in the knowledge that Eli's work here on earth has been fulfilled?"

As Reverend Inman went on to relay touching stories of Eli's ministry, June was painfully aware of Parker's grief. He remained dry eyed, but she knew it was an act of will. People had told her Parker had never supported Eli's work. He came on Sunday to hear him preach on occasion. No doubt to Parker, Eli was a loyal friend who had been plucked from Parker's life too soon, and he saw no purpose or meaning in such a loss.

June's thoughts returned to Reverend Inman's compelling voice.

"Together we will carry on Eli's dream, the dream he so fervently shared with me. We will build the tabernacle. With God's help, we will erect this monument." Isaac wiped his eyes, then continued. "Shall we worry how we'll carry on? No, Eli would say no. Far more important, God says no. 'Thou wilt keep him in perfect peace, whose mind is stayed on thee: because he trusteth in thee,' it says in Isaiah 26:3. Jesus admonishes us not to let our hearts be troubled or afraid. That implies we have a choice in the matter. 'These things I have spoken unto you, that in me ye might have peace. In the world ye shall have tribulation: but be of good cheer; I have overcome the world,' John 16:33.

"Eli Messenger was a gifted man, a man who asked for little here on earth, but a man who is rich beyond measure in the treasure he has laid up for himself in heaven. He was a man who asked little *for* himself, but asked much *of* himself. He offered cool water to the thirsty, comfort to the sorrowing, hope to the hopeless. Friends, 'let not your hearts be troubled,' " Reverend Inman repeated softly. "Together we toil on. Together we will plant seeds and reap the harvest. 'I can do all things through Christ which strengtheneth me,' Philippians 4:13."

Tears rolled down his cheeks now.
"Brother Eli sits at the feet of God today.
He is feasting at the table of the Lord.
And he is hearing God say, 'Well done,
good and faithful servant.' "

Bowing his head, he prayed. "Father, let
our tears be of joy rather than of frustration. Let us move on, glorifying your
name, building your kingdom. For the
days allotted us here upon earth are precious and few."

Lifting his hand, he intoned, "Now, may
the peace of God which passeth all understanding keep our hearts and minds
through Jesus Christ. Amen, and amen."

June lowered her eyes as mourners
rose and began to file silently past Eli's
casket. Reverend Inman had requested
that Eli be buried in a peaceful valley on
the grounds where the tabernacle would
be erected. In his words, "Eli will still be a
part of the dream."

Later, June stood with the other mourners as the pine box was slowly lowered
into a gaping hole in the muddy ground.
When she saw tears unabashedly rolling
down Parker's cheeks, she leaned closer,
pressing a clean handkerchief into his

right hand. He took it, refusing to meet her eyes. Her heart ached for his pain.

"Dust to dust," Reverend Inman intoned softly. "We are all but dust. Brother Eli, you will be sorely missed, but by your devotion you have given us a measure to live up to; by your faith you have given us a light, and by your faithfulness you have given us courage and a greater conviction toward the work we have yet to accomplish."

June wept openly, feeling more than ever that she was called to be a part of something miraculous. Something destined to be a lasting tribute to God, to Eli and Reverend Inman, and, yes, even to Papa, for generations to come.

At the moment, she asked for no more.

Chapter Four

It was settled. June would stay on in Seattle and help raise funds for the tabernacle.

As she dressed the following morning, June thought about the conversation she'd had with Reverend Inman over supper the night before.

"I want to stay on and work to see Eli's dream realized."

Reverend Inman had laid his napkin aside, obviously surprised by her decision. "I thought you would want to return to Michigan."

"No. No," she repeated more softly. "I thought God brought me here to Seattle to marry a wonderful man. Now that Eli's gone, I feel God has a more defined purpose. You know my papa was a pastor.''

Reverend Inman nodded. ''So Eli said.''

''Well, Papa never so much as thought about building anything so grand as a tabernacle, but I believe he would approve of your and Eli's dream. When Eli told me about the dream you and he shared, something moved in my heart, Reverend Inman. Something so deep and so profound that I believe God wants me to stay here, to do all I can to help carry on Eli's work.''

Leaning back in his chair, Reverend Inman appeared to weigh her suggestion. ''You're most welcome to stay if you feel this is where God is leading you. The ministry can use all the hands we can get.''

June could see he was touched that she had caught Eli's vision. ''I've prayed about it, and I believe this is what I am to do. In a small way I'll be doing it for Papa, too. I think he would be proud of my being part of such a grand endeavor.''

''Then, of course, you must stay. Might I hope you will remain here at the complex?''

June nodded. "If that would be all right with you."

"I would have it no other way." He patted her hand. "Oh, my dear, you are indeed a godsend. Eli would be overjoyed to know that you're carrying on in his footsteps."

June sighed, pushing her half-empty plate aside. "Do you think Eli knows, Reverend Inman?"

Reverend Inman smiled. "I think Eli's joy knows no bounds, my dear. Could we ask for anything more?"

"No, nothing more," she agreed. "I thought I would begin tomorrow morning. I have an idea for raising funds I would like to talk over, if I may."

"Certainly." Reverend Inman reached for his coffee. "What's this idea you have?"

His eyes widened as she chatted on. He stirred four teaspoons of sugar into his coffee instead of his usual two, his jaw slackening on occasion. When she was finished, he took a fortifying sip of coffee and leaned back in his chair.

"Well." He cleared his throat. "It is a most uncommon approach, but I can think

of nothing scripturally wrong with it—provided you in no way imply the men should
give out of guilt.''

"Oh, no! I would never imply that. Giving should be from the heart—a freewill
offering. It's just, that's where so many
men go—and I think they'll be happy to
donate to the tabernacle if given an opportunity.''

"Well, they could attend services
nightly," Reverend Inman pointed out.

"Yes, but they don't, Reverend. So I'll
go to them.''

The following afternoon June stood in
front of the saloon, gazing up at the large,
crudely constructed sign nailed to a
weathered-looking shack.

The Gilded Hen looked downright sinful.

She shook her head, wondering if Eli
would have approved of her scheme.
More important, would God object? Reverend Inman had said he could think of no
scriptural reason not to. . . .

Piano music spilled through the double
swinging doors as she balanced on
tiptoes to peek in. Scruffy men sat around

tables playing cards while others stood at the bar and flirted with scantily dressed women with flaming rouged cheeks. Oh, the shame of it all. What would Aunt Thalia say about such goings-on?

When June first thought about a plan to raise funds for the tabernacle, the saloon had immediately come to mind. She and Reverend Inman had driven past the establishment the day he met her ship. Stationed beside the door of The Gilded Hen, she could sing and ring a bell. When the men started home after a long night of drinking and . . . well, whatever a man did in an establishment like The Gilded Hen, she could offer them an opportunity to contribute to a worthwhile community project. If they didn't want to give, they didn't have to. Nothing ventured, nothing gained, Aunt Thalia would say.

Positioning herself to the left of the wood porch, June hummed a few practice notes, then began to sing "Amazing Grace" in a strong, clear alto. The tones were as sweet and pure as the message. Ringing the tiny silver bell, she flashed passersby her sweetest smile. "Donations for the Isaac Inman Crusade! Would you care to give?"

A passing matron responded immediately. "The Isaac Inman Crusade thanks you, and God thanks you," June said as the woman dropped a coin into the cup and walked on.

"Thank you, sir. God bless you."

"Thank you."

"Your kindness is deeply appreciated."

By the end of the first hour she'd emptied the cup once and sung "Amazing Grace" fourteen times. Her mouth was as dry as the floor of a chicken coop, but she'd collected five dollars and twenty-two cents for the Inman Crusade.

Darkness closed around her, and the wind picked up. Huddling deeper into her wool cloak, she rang the bell, keeping an eye on the saloon doorway. The door swung open, and a group of men emerged, holding on to each other for support.

Straightening, she sang louder, "that saaaaaved a wretch like meeeeee. I once was lost . . ."

The men stumbled down the steps, barely sparing her a glance.

She watched them walk on down the street, then eyed the half-empty cup. Drats. The door opened again, and two large men—loggers, she assumed by the impressive width of their shoulders—teetered out.

Lifting the bell, she rang it harder, extending the tin cup. "Can you spare a coin for the Isaac Inman Crusade, sir?"

"For what?" One man stopped to focus on her.

"For the Isaac Inman Crusade. Reverend Inman intends to build a tabernacle right here in Seattle—the likes of which you've never seen." She smiled, holding the cup a little closer. "Can you spare a coin?"

The man leaned unsteadily against the saloon wall, squinting at her.

"The Isaac Inman Crusade," June repeated. "Donations are gratefully appreciated."

He finally focused. "What's yer name, girlie?"

"June, sir."

The two men obediently fished in their pockets and came up with a few coins. Dropping them into the cup, they draped their arms around each other's shoulders and teetered on. She could hear their deep voices singing in disjointed harmony:

> *"Oh, in 1869 in the merry month of*
> *June,*
> *I landed in a vanzousi one sultry*
> *afternoon,*
> *Up stepped a walking skeleton with*
> *his long and lantern jaw. . . ."*

"God bless you, sirs!" June called.

"Well, well. Now, what's your name?" a man sporting the remains of his supper in his unkempt white beard asked a while later.

"God's emissary!" June replied, holding out the cup.

The man gave generously, but his unwarranted winks and ribald remarks brought a blush to June's cheeks. Blowing on her icy fingertips, she thought about calling it a day. Donations had been good, and evening services would be starting soon. Reverend Inman would be delighted when she dropped the day's contributions into the offering plate. The men, for the most part, had given from the heart, pausing occasionally to ask her to remember them in her prayers.

She turned to look over her shoulder when she heard hoofbeats approaching. A huge man rode up and swung out of the saddle, tossing the reins around the hitching post. June frowned when she recognized Parker Sentell.

A shiver raced up her spine. What was he doing at The Gilded Hen?

She had no explanation for what happened next. It was if an invisible force gave her a shove from behind. As the big logger stepped onto the saloon porch, she blocked his path. Her gaze collided with his silver belt buckle, then lifted to follow the long, long row of buttons on his shirt. The man was as tall as a mountain! Lifting the bell, she rang it. "Care to spare a coin, sir?"

Taken off guard, Parker stepped back. June grinned as recognition, then disbelief, dawned in his eyes. She lowered the cup. "Good evening, Mr. Sentell."

Parker eyed her sternly. "What are you doing in a place like this?"

"Collecting donations." She shook the

cup, and the coins jangled. "They've been quite good. Care to make a contribution?"

His scowl reminded her of her childhood and Aunt Thalia's disapproving looks. He stepped around her, and she resumed her position by the steps. She didn't care if she annoyed him. Now maybe he would realize she was serious about her intentions to carry out Eli's work. Jingling the tin cup, she called, "Donations for the Isaac Inman Crusade!"

A logger dropped a coin into the cup and walked on.

"God bless you!"

Giving her a look of pained tolerance, Parker pushed through the doorway and disappeared into the saloon.

Anxious to see what he was doing, she scrambled to the swinging doors and peeked inside. Parker stood at a table of young men playing cards. They looked to be very young—no more than early teens. Towering over the boys, the logger issued a few curt words. Chairs overturned as the boys darted toward the door.

June jumped back to avoid being trampled as the four burst out and struck off down the middle of the street in a dead run.

Wow! What had Parker said? Whatever it was, she was glad it hadn't been directed at her.

Her curiosity got the better of her, and she stepped back to the doorway. The sound of heavy boots hitting hardwood floor met her ears as Parker forcefully strode out, almost bowling her over. Stumbling, she reached out to grasp the railing.

Giving her a hard look, he walked down the steps, reached for the reins, got on his horse, and rode off.

Leaning against the rail, she took a deep breath, sourly eyeing his disappearing horse. He was such an unpleasant man.

Thirty-five dollars and sixty-two cents for the tabernacle. June lay back on her bed and stared at the ceiling, exhausted. She'd been in Seattle a little over two weeks, and already she was well on the way to helping Reverend Inman and Eli achieve their goal. Her heart sang with accomplishment. The only damper on her enthusiasm was Parker Sentell. What would it take to make him warm up to her? His continuing aloofness was like ice water on her joy.

Until she came to Seattle, June had never been more than fifty miles in any direction outside of Cold Water.

Now she was hundreds of miles from home, separated from family, close friends, and the only life she'd ever known. Everything that once felt safe and familiar suddenly seemed to have existed eons ago.

Even with her efforts to raise funds, she found it difficult to fill the hours in the day. She spent late afternoons and early evenings in front of The Gilded Hen, but days like these, when the skies poured down heavy rains, prevented her from going at all.

She clung to the belief that God had sent her to help with Reverend Inman's ministry. With Eli gone, God surely must mean for her to carry out the important work Eli had started.

One minute she was certain, or at least

practically certain, that she was destined to remain in Washington.

The next minute she definitely knew, or at least was pretty sure, that she should return to Michigan.

Maybe if she talked to Reverend Inman about her jumbled feelings, he could help with the many questions that burdened her heart.

Above all, she desperately wanted to do the right thing. If only the Lord would speak to her spirit and grant her guidance and wisdom, she would gladly follow wherever he led.

Full of determination to do better, she headed for Reverend Inman's room late Monday morning. When she arrived, however, he was gone.

"If you're lookin' for the reverend, he's . . . he's not here," a childish voice informed her.

Startled, June looked around to see who was speaking.

Ben Wilson, a crusade usher, was sweeping the hallway with a large broom. Ben, a thin, big-boned man, towered over the heads of other men who worked with the crusade.

Fellow workers good-naturedly teased Ben that he was as slow as molasses. Rudy Silas, Ben's best friend, quickly spoke up and said that whatever Ben lacked upstairs he made up for with his unshakable willingness to do God's work.

June had silently agreed, wishing that she'd had the courage to speak in Ben's defense. Ben was a little odd at times, but he was a kind man. She recognized his total devotion to the Lord and felt a kindred spirit with Ben Wilson from the moment she met him.

"Hello, Ben." June smiled and smoothed her dark blue wool skirt in place.

"Hey, Miss June." Ben shuffled his big boots against the floor.

"Do you know where I might find Reverend Inman?"

"Yes."

A moment of silence passed without Ben's saying.

"Can you tell me?" June prompted.

"Yes," Ben said, raking a calloused hand through his thick gray hair.

"Where, then, is Reverend Inman?"

"The reverend went to Sea—Sea—

Sea—'' Ben's face throbbed a bright red as he struggled to pronounce the words.

"Seattle?"

"Yes, Miss June. That's where he went." Ben grinned, revealing a missing front tooth.

"Did he say how long he'd be gone?"

"Yes."

"How long will he be gone, Ben?" June asked patiently.

"Said he'd be gone 'til dark." Ben's eyes glowed with pride. Sometimes Ben forgot things. June could see his self-esteem elevate, if only briefly, from having remembered the reverend's promise.

"Hey, Ben!" A man stuck his head around the corridor doorway. "Buddy, we need your help outside."

"I'm their buddy," Ben said. His smile widened. "They need me."

"Thank you for your help, Ben." June smiled as Ben put on his hat.

"You're welcome, Miss June." The big man headed toward the door, reminding himself with pride, "They need you. You have to go, Ben. They need you."

June watched out the window as Ben pitched in to help erect a large pole. He was eager to work, doing anything, from the dirtiest, heaviest tasks to running the simplest errands. All anyone had to do was tell Ben where he was needed.

Sighing, she focused on the large crusade tent. What should she do with all her time? The crusade had all the services it needed. People came from far and wide to hear Reverend Inman preach.

June admired the landscape lining the crusade ground. Trees, tall and majestic. As far as the eye could see, trees.

Trees . . .

Lumber . . .

Lumber camps . . .

Lumberjacks . . .

Families of lumberjacks . . .

Parker said men had to wait until spring breakup to see their families, but surely there were a few women and children privileged to live with their men.

Services.

"That's it!" June shouted. She quickly glanced over her shoulder to see if anyone had heard her. Ettie was nowhere to be seen. The building was deserted this morning.

Her direction was now clear to her. How

could she have missed the obvious?
Gathering the folds of her wool skirt, she
hurried toward the area where Ben was
working. She knew exactly what she
wanted to do. Big, rowdy lumberjacks
rarely came to the crusade meetings.
Some promised to attend services, telling
her they would do so for "God's little emissary." Five actually came one night, but
she was still waiting for the others.

The way she figured it, their wives and
children would enjoy informal services if
the services were brought to them.

Her hope spiraled downward.

The plan would obligate her to deal with
Parker Sentell. He ran the largest camp
around and oversaw four others. She
wouldn't be able to go into those camps
without his knowledge. She sat for a moment and thought about the problem. Re-
solve stiffened her shoulders. God's work
was more important than her rocky rela-
tionship with Parker Sentell.

Enthused by her plan, she hurried to
find Ben. He was busy helping a fellow
worker pick up leaflets in the crusade tent.
She drew him aside so they could speak
privately.

"I need your help."

Ben's face lit from ear to ear. "Miss June needs my help?"

In no time at all, the man with the intelligence of a ten-year-old had the buggy hitched and waiting. He carefully helped June climb aboard the driver's seat.

"Thank you, Ben." June reached for his hand and squeezed it. "You're a true gentleman."

"Miss June is welcome." Ben grinned, his eyes brightening. "I am a gentle man."

"That you are." June picked up the reins. "Ben, please tell Reverend Inman I'll be back before dark."

He nodded and returned to his earlier task. June heard him reciting, "Back before dark. Back before dark."

She drove directly to Pine Ridge. She wasn't sure how to approach Parker about holding services in the camp, but with a hefty measure of the Lord's help, she would think of something.

She'd never seen such spectacular beauty. The deepest green pines, the bluest sky, the most vivid browns dotted the meadows. As she traveled deeper into the piney forest, she noticed the path nar-

rowed to bumpy ruts. The route must be
one of many logging roads cut through
the heart of the woods. The ground beneath the towering trees was blanketed
with a cushion of ferns. She smiled, recalling the briars she had endured as a child,
racing through Cold Water's brambly
groves.

A bend appeared in the road, and June
spotted the sign proclaiming Pine Ridge
Logging Camp. Reining the horse to a
stop, she sat for a moment, collecting her
thoughts. God as yet hadn't given her the
insight about how to approach Parker.
Well, maybe at this point she wasn't supposed to know. Perhaps this was a time
when the Lord wanted her to travel by
faith, not by her instincts, which more
often than not proved to be troublesome.

If only she had started off on better
footing with the obstinate logger, she
wouldn't be facing this uphill battle. There
must be something good about the man;
she just had to find it.

Five minutes later June stopped the
buggy in front of a small log building. *Pine
Ridge Company Store,* she read.

The sound of razor-sharp axes biting

into wood echoed through camp. The rhythmical grind of crosscut saws, or, as Papa had called them, misery whips, filled the air. In the distance a logging road ran parallel to the forest. Teams of mules labored to drag heavy loads of logs chained to a skid. Somewhere deep within the woods, a man shouted a warning. The next thing June knew, the ground beneath her shook from the weight of a felled tree. The jolt spooked the horse.

Holding tightly to the reins, she struggled to control the animal, yet it was obvious that it was only a matter of time before the frightened horse overcame her weakening grip. Her arms burned as she wrestled with the reins.

In the midst of the frenzy, she glimpsed Parker darting from the camp office. His long legs effortlessly covered the ground as he raced toward the swaying buggy. The horse whinnied and reared on its hind legs, threatening to overturn the small conveyance.

Parker's hand snaked out and grasped the bridle, putting him dangerously close to the animal's powerful hooves. Gripping the leather, he calmed the wild beast.

"Whoa, girl. Easy, there."

The animal pranced wide eyed and gradually responded to his soothing tone.

June was shaking. Meeting Parker's stern gaze, she smiled weakly.

"Are you OK?" Parker walked around the horse, giving the animal a gentle pat. It took a moment for June to compose herself.

"Yes . . . thank you—I didn't realize the horse would spook so easily." She touched her hand to her hair. Well, she'd certainly made a fool of herself! "I don't like to think what might have happened if you hadn't come to my rescue."

Parker crossed his arms and stared at her. "That's what I'm here for."

She was relieved that he seemed to be in a better mood than at their previous meeting. She tried to move, but couldn't. "I think I'm paralyzed."

Before she realized it, he had lifted her down from the buggy. The strength in his arms amazed her.

Their gaze touched briefly, and he set her gently on her feet. She quickly looked away. "Your camp . . . it's very nice. I forgot to mention that on my last visit."

Parker studied the long, neat row of bunkhouses as if seeing them for the first time. "The men work long hours; they deserve a decent place to live."

"You should be congratulated." Other logging camps she'd seen in the area weren't as nice. Most looked as if they'd been thrown together with spit and baling wire. Parker took her arm and steered her toward the office. "I don't suppose you came all the way out here to comment on the condition of my camp."

Color flooded June's face. "No, I didn't."

"Then to what exactly do I owe the pleasure of this visit?"

"Well, first of all, I'd like for us to be friends." There. She'd said it. Bold as brass. He could either recognize her attempt to reconcile their differences, or they could continue at sword's point. She'd much prefer the former. "I think we've gotten off to a bad start, and I want to apologize if it's my fault."

He simply stared at her, weighing the offer. After a moment he said, "All right. Apology accepted. I guess I owe you one too." He extended his hand, his smile almost pleasant. "I have nothing against you, Miss Kallahan. I don't approve of the tabernacle or your part in it. But, I'm willing to let bygones be bygones."

She smiled, tremendously relieved. They shook on it. His grip was firm and confident.

"Now, Miss Kallahan. What's on your mind this afternoon?"

Drawing a deep breath, she said quietly, "I have a proposition for you."

His eyes narrowed. "A what?"

"A proposition. Interested in hearing it?"

"Should I be?"

"Yes. I think so." He smiled, and she suddenly felt flushed. The sun was warmer than expected. She needed to remove her cloak.

"Why am I almost certain I *don't* want to hear this proposition?"

"You may not, but I'm going to present it anyway."

Recrossing his arms, his guarded blue eyes studied her. "I'm listening."

June quickly tried to choose the best approach to argue her request. She needed to be tactful. She didn't want to scare him off her idea. "I understand you oversee many of the logging camps in the area?''

He conceded with a nod. ''A few.''

''The work must be very arduous.''

''Most work is.''

''Long days—the men are worn by the end of the week—much too weary to travel much farther than the bunkhouse.''

''You looking for work?''

He wasn't making her job any easier, but she didn't discourage easily. ''No, but I've noticed that not many loggers attend revival services.''

He shook his head, shifting his stance. ''Not many.''

''Well—I've been thinking that perhaps the men's wives and children would like services—maybe even some of the men would, if services were brought to them.''

He stared down at her with his arms folded across his chest in a fighter's stance. ''That's what you think.''

Taking a deep breath, she continued, ''That's what I think—and I'm also thinking there's no reason they should be deprived of services when I am quite willing to provide them.''

It seemed to take a moment for her implication to sink in. When it did, his eyes narrowed. "Are you asking to set up a tent revival here? In camp?"

"Oh, no," June assured him. "Nothing like that. Just an informal Sunday service—"

"No."

Her jaw dropped. "But you haven't heard—"

"I've heard all I need to hear." He shifted positions, and June could see a stubborn set forming along his jawline. "We've gotten along fine without outside services; there's no reason to start one now."

"Mr. Sentell—"

"I didn't say we don't have services; I said we don't have *outside* services."

She eyed him skeptically. "You have services?"

"Hoss Barlow reads a couple of Scriptures before breakfast Sunday mornings."

"A couple of Scriptures? You call that services?"

"The amount of Scripture isn't a problem with God; why should it be a problem for you?"

June's confidence was shaken, but not

her spirit. "Every man, woman, and child should keep the Sabbath holy. The men, especially, need to hear more than 'a couple of Scriptures.' I'm sure—"

"You haven't been here long enough to be sure of anything." He straightened, his arms dropping back to his sides. "But I have, and I want no part of Isaac Inman's Evangelistic Crusades *or* his tabernacle. I thought I made that clear."

June opened her mouth to argue, but he stopped her.

"What Isaac does on crusade ground is his business. Pine Ridge is my business. We don't need you coming in here, stirring up trouble under the guise of Sunday services."

"Mr. Sentell!"

He lifted an imperious brow, his eyes issuing her a challenge. "I'll tell you the same thing I told Eli. There are far greater needs, Miss Kallahan. Open your eyes and look around you. Now, if you'll excuse me, I don't believe we have anything more to discuss. I have work to do—unless, of course, you can't find your way back to Inman's camp, in which case I'll have one of my men drive you."

Why—the man had more gall than starched long johns! June straightened, refusing to let him shake her. "I am perfectly capable of driving myself back, thank you."

"I'm sure you are." Parker turned and walked off. Seething, she watched him disappear into the office and shut the door.

So that was it. He was mad at Reverend Inman. Eli had said as much, but if Parker thought for one moment his mean spirit would deter her work for the tabernacle, he had another think coming. His obstinacy only made her that much more determined to succeed. She *would* start Sunday services for women and children—if not at Pine Ridge, then at some other camp—with or without his approval.

Logging camps were all alike. The needs were the same, and she felt now, more than ever, that leading a morning worship service was something she needed to do. The Lord said to pick up the cross and follow him. He didn't say it would always be easy to carry or that she wouldn't meet any Parker Sentells along the way.

Climbing back into the buggy, she spotted a lumberjack leaving Parker's office. Springing to her feet, she called out, "Sir? Excuse me. Can you help me?"

The man glanced up, smiling. June shivered. All the men in this camp were giants. This one was even taller than Parker Sentell, if that was possible.

As the logger approached, she encountered a pair of earnest brown eyes. When he spoke, the manly rumble made her think of rich, warm honey. "Yes, ma'am?"

"Where's the next nearest logging camp?"

He paused, glancing toward the west. "Tin Cup, about a mile up the road."

Smiling, she turned the buggy. "Thank you!"

"Ma'am," he called, "you don't want to go there! It's no place for a lady—"

"Thank you," she called gaily. "But it's exactly where this lady wants to go!"

Chapter Five

The buggy rattled along the rutted road, jarring June's skull. Surely the kind lumberjack had pointed her in the wrong direction. *Might as well turn back. But . . . perhaps it's just around the next bend. . . .*

As she debated with herself, she finally spotted an obscured, weathered sign reading "Tin Cup."

Breathing a sigh of relief, June trotted the horse through the crudely built log arch.

The difference between Pine Ridge and Tin Cup was shocking. A foul odor met her nose and stung her eyes. As the buggy rolled farther into camp, she was sickened by the deplorable living conditions.

Moldering garbage dumps fouled the air with a rotting stench. Trash littered the ground—slivers of broken bottles, discarded tins, and pieces of broken furniture. Pigs and dogs ran loose. Chickens roosted on housetops.

Houses consisted of ragged tents and unkempt shacks. The area reminded June of the aftermath of a bad storm that had once torn through Cold Water.

The buggy rolled deeper into camp. June saw a small, barefoot boy dart out, shouting at the top of his lungs, "Stranger's a-comin'!" The child quickly ducked back into one of the shacks, where a woman peered curiously from behind tattered curtains. When June looked her way, she quickly allowed the material to drop back into place.

The camp was eerily quiet for a Monday. No piercing saws or rattling chains, or logs rolling toward the river. June glanced over her shoulder as the sound of men's laughter, tongues thick with drink, floated from a nearby tent.

She swallowed. What *was* this place?

Whirling to look behind her, June considered turning the buggy in search of a more civilized camp.

A man's head suddenly appeared in the opening of the tent flap. His frowning glance swept the camp, coming to a halt on June and the buggy. His eyes narrowed.

June's heart pounded. Gripping the reins, she ran her tongue over her dry lips. She had made a huge mistake. She should have listened to the logger who had warned her not to come. She jumped at a surly voice.

"You want somethin'?"

The tall, skinny man, his beard thick with tobacco spittle, studied her. Her heart hammered against her ribs. Where had he come from?

He stepped closer. "I'd be more than happy to accommodate."

A second logger approached; he was almost as big around as he was tall. Five or six huge, dirty men drifted out of the tent. Their eyes greedily assessed her.

Please, God, June prayed silently. *Make my words bold.*

"Well, sir, I'm . . . I'm here for a purpose." She cleared her throat, trying to think of it. "I've come to bring you good news!"

Please, God, let them consider Sunday services good news!

"What good news?" The skinny man eyed her up and down, then bent at the waist to hawk up a wad of tobacco.

"Very good news." She tried to smile confidently. "Wonderful news."

A man pushed his way to the front of the crowd. He was so slovenly that the smell of him reached the buggy before he did. "What do you want, woman? Spit it out."

June turned away from the stench and silently implored God to give her strength. "I've come to offer you services—Sunday services—for you and your families—"

The men's laughter overpowered her faint voice. She glanced from man to man. Scraggly beards, dirty hands with nails bitten and broken to the quick, clothes that reeked of unwashed bodies. Should she turn around and leave?

She summoned the courage to continue. Her voice rose. "I want to come to your camp on Sunday mornings and share with you and your families preaching, prayer, Bible study, singing—"

The rounded man approached the buggy, fingering the hem of her blue wool skirt. He leered at her. "What is it you're offering to share, little lady?"

The men broke into laughter, elbowing each other.

June reached out and firmly removed the man's fingers, determined to keep her head. She had done a foolish thing. She couldn't afford another mistake. Staring straight ahead, she reiterated her intent. "I am with the Isaac Inman Crusade. I'm here this morning to see if your camp is in need of Sunday services—"

"You're one of those preacher women? One of those crusaders?"

The men roared. "That's a good one!" someone called.

"She's here to see if we need any churchin'! What say, men?" A man held out his suspenders, winking. "Do we need any churchin'?"

Leaning back in his chair, Parker stared out the office window. For some reason he couldn't shake the thought of the morning's visitor.

He was surprised at how quickly June had given up. He didn't know her well, but he did know she was pushy and somewhat naive. He'd gotten the feeling that she wasn't easily swayed from a purpose. So why hadn't she tried harder to persuade him to hold services at the camp? His gut feeling told him that deep within June Kallahan there burned a fire that would not easily be extinguished.

"Parker, I need your signature on these documents. There's a shipment of new saws due out of Seattle first thing tomorrow morning." Simon Hendricks handed his boss a stack of papers.

Drawn from his thoughts, Parker looked up. "What?" he asked absently.

Parker's clerk rattled the sheaf of papers. "Your signature? On these?"

"The new saws?"

"The new saws. Where's your mind today?"

Parker leaned across the desk and took the papers. His mind was on June Kallahan, Eli's mail-order bride. With Eli gone, she should go back to Michigan. His jaw tensed when he thought about her declaration that she wanted to see Eli's dream realized. He mentally snorted. Eli's dream—building that tabernacle was Isaac's dream, a dream to glorify Isaac's work. If Inman wanted a cause to promote, he need look no further than the poverty in the area. Families going hungry, the orphanage where children were going without proper food and clothing. That old woman, Angeline, who was trying to raise a houseful of kids with no help except that old Indian. Inman's "tabernacle" wasn't going to put food in folks' bellies, or shoes on those orphans' feet.

"Is something wrong, boss?" Simon eyed him with a concerned frown.

Parker leaned back, stretching. "Nothing's wrong. Just a little tired, I guess." But something was wrong. Something nagged at him.

Simon's hand was on the doorknob when Parker stopped him. Something told him not to ask, that he didn't really want to know. Common sense dictated he'd better.

"Did I see you talking to the Kallahan girl earlier?"

"The woman in the buggy?" Simon nodded his head warily.

Parker's heart sank. Simon had a heart of gold. If *he* was worried, Parker's instincts were on target.

"She wanted to know where the nearest camp was. I told her she didn't want to go there, but—"

Parker slammed his fist on the desk and got up. "Blast that woman!"

"Trouble, boss?"

"Saddle the horses, Simon."

"Right away." Simon hurried out the door, pulling on his coat.

Parker took a deep breath. June was naive, but was she crazy? Riding into Tin Cup, spouting the gospel? They'd have her for supper. For a moment he considered letting her learn the hard way. Going off, half cocked, to a camp known for its . . .

Reaching for his coat, he shrugged into the fleece lining. Regardless of his aggravation, he couldn't allow anything to happen to her. Loyalty to Eli, as well as his own judgment, forbade it.

"Gonna preach to us, girlie?"

Trying desperately to hide her fear, June swallowed hard. Intent on drowning out the suggestive words of the vulgar men, she turned Papa's words over in her mind. *The Lord will take what the enemy has intended for harm and turn it to good.*

"Well, now, yo're a purty li'l thing, ain't ya!" A burly man grinned up at her, showing rotting teeth. "All dressed up and smellin' so fine!"

Fear is not of God. Fear is not of God, June told herself. Springing to her feet, June pointed a commanding finger at the man as he closed in. "You stop right there!"

"Fiery, too!"

In her mind Papa's voice, clear as a bell, shouted, *Sing, June! Sing!*

June opened her mouth and belted out one of the songs she'd sung in front of the saloon yesterday.

> *"We give Thee but thine own,*
> *Whate'er the gift may be:*
> *All that we have is Thine alone,*
> *A trust, O Lord, from Thee."*

The words tumbled out crisp and clear. From the corner of her eye she saw the men were listening.

"May we Thy bounties thus
As stewards true receive,
And gladly, as Thou blessest us,
To Thee our first fruits give."

Two men slowly removed their hats and laid them over their hearts.

"O hearts are bruised and dead,
And homes are bare and cold,
And lambs for whom the Shepherd bled
Are straying from the fold."

June's knees were knocking so hard that she thought the men would surely hear it. She silently thanked God for the power of song and her singing voice. Without this talent, she would surely be thrown over one of these bullies' shoulders and hauled off to who knew where. She shuddered, and sang louder.

"To comfort and to bless,
To find a balm for woe,

To tend the lone and fatherless,
Is angels' work below.

"The captive to relieve,
To God the lost to bring,
To teach the way of life and peace—
It is a Christlike thing.

"And we believe Thy word,
Though dim our faith may be:
Whate'er for Thine we do, O Lord—"

She glanced at the men and finished
with a rush.

"We do it unto Thee."

She was running out of verses! Now
what should she do?

"I have found a friend in Jesus, He's
everything to me,
He's the fairest of ten thousand to my
soul;
The 'Lily of the Valley,' in Him alone I
see,
All I need to cleanse and make me
fully whole.

In sorrow He's my comfort, in trouble
He's my stay,
He tells me every care on Him to roll;
He's the 'Lily of the Valley, the Bright
and Morning Star,'
He's the fairest of ten thousand to my
soul—"

She wavered at the sound of approaching hoofbeats, going limp with relief when she saw Parker Sentell gallop into camp, along with the giant she'd asked directions from earlier.

Parker shot her a look that told her he was angry with her, but even with his caustic glance, June was relieved to see him.

The men cleared a wide path for the big Pine Ridge foreman. June dropped weakly to the buggy seat. Her knees were so watery that she hoped he wouldn't ask her to get out of the buggy.

The man who had grabbed her hem grinned. "Howdy, Mr. Sentell."

Parker nodded to the camp foreman. "Herschal." His eyes scanned the group of rough men. "What's going on here?"

"Just singin', Mr. Sentell."

Parker gave him a dubious look. "Singing?"

Herschal hung his head. "Aw, me and the boys was jest havin' fun with the little lady. Don't mean no harm."

Parker glanced at June, then back to Herschal. "Then I suggest you apologize to the lady."

Herschal whipped off his hat, nervously twisting the dingy brim in his fingertips. "Sorry, missy."

"The lady's name is Miss Kallahan."

Herschal shot Parker a pained look, then tried again. "Sorry, Miss Kallahan. Didn't mean no harm."

Parker dismissed Herschal with a cold look and turned to June. She swallowed, feeling like a disobedient child caught in the act and about to be punished.

His eyes pinned her. "Shouldn't you be getting back?"

Afraid to further aggravate him, June nodded. Giving Herschal a withering glance, she turned the buggy and followed Parker and Simon out.

When they reached the arch, Parker motioned for her to follow him back to Pine Ridge. She caught her lower lip between her teeth and bit down, wondering about the wisdom of obeying. She would probably be well advised to keep going, but she couldn't. After all, he had rescued her from a frightening encounter.

During the brief ride back to Pine Ridge, she counted her blessings and thanked God for his protection—even if it *had* come in the form of Parker Sentell.

When Parker swung off the black stallion, he handed the reins to a shantyboy. Then he turned to his assistant. "Simon, please stay with our 'guest' until I can figure out what to do."

Simon nodded. "Yes, sir."

Parker stalked into his office and went to his desk. Blast that Miss Kallahan! She was a burr in his side. Stubborn as all get-out. He had been right—she didn't give up easily.

He sighed. It wasn't that he really minded if she brought the loggers services—Lord knew, it might do the men good. He just couldn't stand the thought of connecting his men in any way with Isaac Inman's crusade. Now, if she would

take a collection for the orphans, that
would be a different story. But she was so
set on carrying on Eli's dream, he was
sure she would be just as blind to other
needs as Isaac was.

He looked out the window at her. She
sat quietly in the buggy, waiting for his
decision. Why didn't she go back to Michigan, where she belonged? In spite of
himself, he felt a sense of responsibility for
her while she remained in Seattle. Out of
loyalty to Eli, he couldn't let anything happen to her. And he had to admit that Eli
probably would have been proud of her
for what she wanted to do.

Expelling a heavy breath, he shoved his
chair back from the desk and bellowed
out the door. "Simon!"

"Yes, boss?"

"Get in here!"

"Yes, sir!" Simon left his post beside
the buggy and strode to the office.

Parker stood at his desk. "What do you
think of this cockamamy idea of hers?"

"You want my honest opinion?"

"I don't expect you to humor me."

"I think you're wrong . . . about this
Sunday service thing."

Parker nodded. "Go on."

"I think women and children, and some of the men as well, would appreciate a Sunday service. I know I would."

"Are you willing to accompany her to every service and see that she doesn't get into trouble?"

"Yes, sir, I'd be willing to do that."

Parker rubbed his chin, staring in June's direction. "I'd just as soon ship her home as deal with her."

"Yes, sir, but you can't."

Getting up from the desk, Parker moved to the window and stared out. Much as he hated to do it, he knew what he had to do. Finally he turned around to Simon. "Ask Miss Kallahan to step in here."

Simon appeared in the doorway, meeting June's apprehensive gaze. He grinned. "Boss wants to see you."

Gathering her skirts, she climbed down from the wagon, wondering if Parker intended to make a scene before he gave his permission to hold services. She hoped not. One embarrassment a day was quite enough.

Entering his office, she glanced around at the furnishings. Two battered desks, a stove with a large pipe extending through the ceiling, three wooden chairs, and a battered file cabinet. A big window faced east. "Sit down, Miss Kallahan."

She sank down in one of the wooden chairs, her legs still wobbly from the earlier experience.

As Parker paced the wood floor, hands behind his back, his features remained stoic. She remembered his smile earlier in the day and wished he'd engage in the act a little more often. It softened the tight lines around his mouth.

He paused, facing her. "You are sorely trying my patience."

She slid to the edge of the chair. "I don't mean to. For the life of me, I don't know why I anger you. I'm only trying to help."

"Help?" He snorted. "You're determined to hold these services on Sunday?"

There was no need to bear false witness. His friendship with Eli gave him the right to know her intentions. "Yes, sir, I truly am."

She saw there was disapproval on the

tip of his tongue. He seemed to war with frustration, then continued pacing.

"You're a stubborn woman, Miss Kallahan."

She didn't know what to say about that. She *was* stubborn. Especially when she was forced to defend a cause she strongly believed in, and she believed strongly in Sunday services for camp women and children, whether he did or not.

"Yes, sir. I've been told that before."

He paced to the window, where he stood staring out, hands still behind his back. He was silent for so long that she was certain he'd forgotten her.

Finally he said in a carefully modulated voice, "If you're so all-fired set on doing this, I won't stop you. A man should be allowed to worship on Sunday. But . . ."

His "but" resonated through the room.

"Only if Simon accompanies you to the services."

"Every one of them?"

"Every one in surrounding camps."

Her pulse leaped. The punishment could be worse. From what she'd seen of Simon, the gentle giant would be more than adequate protection and a delight to be around. After today's experience, it was easy to accept Parker's pronouncement.

"Logging camps are no place for single women." Parker turned from the window, meeting her gaze. "Men tend to forget they're in a lady's presence. I warn you, I can't be responsible for the men's language."

"Perhaps after a few services, they'll be more conscious of their shortcomings."

His face remained stony. "I assure you they won't. The first sign of trouble will be the last of your services." His gaze nailed hers. "Do I make myself clear?"

"Quite clear," she conceded. "I won't be any trouble—I hope to be an inspiration."

He laughed as if she'd said something funny.

She laughed back. She'd show him she could be an inspiration if she wanted.

They stared at each other for an uncomfortably long time until June gave in first. Heaving a defeated sigh, she broke eye contact. "Now that we have that out of our systems, I need to thank you."

"For what?"

"For coming to my rescue earlier. I realize I acted foolishly, and I won't be doing that again. And thank you for allowing me to hold services. I thank you, and others will thank you once the services commence."

"I'm not interested in thank-yous, Miss Kallahan. I'm only interested in keeping the peace. I don't have time to be rescuing you from any more situations like we just walked out of."

"I understand, and I promise that you don't have to worry about me. I'll not go anywhere without Simon."

She leaned forward to hear his mumbled words but could only catch the clipped phrases: "flighty women" and "Simon having to spend his Sundays looking after her" and "what was Eli thinking?" Well, anyway, she was happy he was going to cooperate.

"I promise you won't regret it."

He started out of the office, then turned back to face her. Bracing his large hand on the doorframe, he dropped his bombshell. "By the way, while you're in camp, you are not—and I repeat, *not*—to take up a donation for the Inman Crusade. Not one cent, Miss Kallahan."

She opened her mouth to protest, and his censuring look stopped her.

"Not one cent, Miss Kallahan. Do I make myself clear? Nothing for the tabernacle."

Nothing? How could he be so cold? He was within his rights to forbid her to solicit money, but the tabernacle was for the Lord. Couldn't he see that?

Resigned, she nodded. It was his camp, and after all, money wasn't the issue. The issue was bringing the gospel to others, and he was allowing that. She wouldn't ask for more. Like Aunt Thalia said: "Never look a gift horse in the mouth."

"All right. No offering. You have my word."

Nodding, he walked out, leaving her to savor her small-but-nonetheless-sweet victory.

She had a hunch that wouldn't happen often with Parker Sentell.

Chapter Six

The crusade tent was filled to capacity. Benches strained beneath the weight of the faithful who returned night after night. June waited for Reverend Inman to mount the platform and take his seat on the right before she slipped onto one end of a wooden bench toward the back.

Someone toward the front stood up and began the first verse of "Praise Him! Praise Him!" in a clear baritone, which was soon joined by the congregation. The richness of the worshipers' efforts more than made up for the scarcity of musical talent.

By the end of the first chorus, most of

the people were on their feet, lifting their voices toward heaven.

"Praise Him! Praise Him! Jesus, our
*   blessed Redeemer!*
For our sins He suffered, and bled
*   and died.*
He our Rock, our hope of eternal
*   salvation,*
Hail Him! Hail Him! Jesus the Crucified."

Mixed emotions flooded June. Even though she had never attended a meeting with Eli, she felt his presence strongly. She missed him, though she'd known him so briefly. She couldn't help feeling that the work would suffer.

"Love unbounded, wonderful, deep
*   and strong."*

Eli had loved his work, and she'd caught a glimpse of how much he seemed to have loved people. She hoped to fill an infinitesimal part of the gap left by his untimely passing.

She opened her eyes as the voices

blended sweetly into "I Must Tell Jesus,"
a hymn that spoke directly to the heart.

"I must tell Jesus all of my trials
I cannot bear these burdens alone."

Creases etched in careworn faces lifted
toward heaven as each, in his or her own
way, told Jesus a particular trial or burden. What a blessing it was to come together and know that no concern was
ever too small for Jesus to care about.
June found herself questioning why a
godly man like Eli was allowed to die—
She caught herself. Surely Eli would not
want her to question. God was in control.

She drew a resigned breath and slowly
released it. It would dishonor Eli if she,
even for a moment, doubted that his life,
as well as his death, could, and would, be
used by God for the good he intended.

She joined with the chorus, "I must tell
Jesus! I must tell Jesus!"

As the words faded, the crowd fell silent. When the last rustle, the last foot
scrape, had settled, only then did Reverend Inman approach the front of the nar-
row stage. June thought he looked tired

tonight, drawn, as if the weight of the world rested on his shoulders.

His eyes scanned the crowd. Then he spoke. "I quote from Hosea 8:7. 'For they have sown the wind, and they shall reap the whirlwind: it hath no stalk: the bud shall yield no meal: if so be it yield, the strangers shall swallow it up.'"

Rubbing his hand across his face, he continued softly, "It is we, the believers, the ones chosen by God to do his work, who must work for his kingdom. We must build the vessel in which to rescue those who are lost in sin."

June listened to the message, fully understanding why Eli had nearly idolized this dynamic man of God. His words, his reflections, his crisp, clear commands gleaned from the Word brought goose bumps to her arms. He brought heaven down to earth during the ensuing hour and a half.

"And I say unto you: The Lord's work will be done! Will you be there?" Reverend Inman's voice rose to a fever pitch. "Will you be the one to build the vessel? Will you be there to throw out the lifeline?" The crowd swelled to their feet, their voices lifted in praise.

"Throw out the lifeline!
Throw out the lifeline!
Someone is drifting away."

"Will you close your eyes against the light? Will you harden your heart against the work? Or will you help build the tabernacle?" Reverend Inman's voice swept the crowd, bringing men and women to their feet. They continued singing in unison while making their way to the altar. Collection baskets were passed around. People dug deep, tossing coins, some dollars, into the baskets. The Spirit of the Lord was moving, and his people responded with open hearts.

June recalled Eli's glowing praise of Reverend Inman, how he was a visionary, able to see and do great things. He propelled God's people to action. Workers extolled his goodness, his purity of heart. He was a man devoted to God, a man who worked unceasingly to bring hope to the lost and weary.

June dropped a coin into the passing

basket, wishing she could contribute a king's ransom. She'd heard of people who accused Christians of placing too much emphasis on money. Papa once explained that giving was necessary to a Christian's spiritual wellness. God did not need a person's money, but giving for the kingdom was a way his child could become more Christlike and less self-centered. Papa contended that a person's attitude toward giving reflected where his or her heart truly was.

Friday dawned cool and overcast. Pewter gray edged the horizon and promised more rain. As the day wore on, the gray deepened. During the afternoon, June prepared for her visit to the logging camps on the coming Sunday. Filled with the prospect of bringing the gospel to those who were hungry to hear it, she selected Scriptures and fashioned colorful paper chains with Bible verses written on them.

As time for the evening services drew near, the wind picked up. Fingers of lightning embroidered rolling clouds. By five o'clock the lamps were lit in order for people to find their way into the tent.

Hanging lamps oscillated crazily on wooden pegs as the wind battered the tent. Sides and top flapped like a great, angry canvas bird. June pulled her shawl closer as she threaded her way through the milling crowd.

"Good evening, Miss June." Ben doffed his hat when he spotted her, bowing from the waist.

"Good evening, Ben. Looks like we're in for a storm."

Ben's childlike features folded. "Ben don't like storms."

June reached to grasp his hand. His skin was cold and rough from hard work. "Are you frightened?"

Lifting his head, he smiled. "Ben's not afraid. God loves Ben. Ben loves God. My Father tells Ben not to be afraid."

Squeezing his hand, June wondered at his perfect innocence. "With God on our side, who can be against us?"

Ben nodded with childlike zeal. "No one against us when God is for us."

He wandered around, checking each lantern to make certain it was secure in the rising wind. June busied herself with the offering baskets, placing them beneath the correct pews, out of the way but easy to locate by those taking the nightly contribution.

Half an hour before services, there wasn't a seat left. June thought the threatening weather might keep some worshipers away, especially the older citizens and those with younger children, but the faithful didn't let a little rain stop them.

The rumble of thunder accompanied voices lifted in song as Reverend Inman took his seat on the platform. Bright lightning flashes illuminated the tent, and the wind continued to rise, snapping canvas in time with the beat of the song. Ben and other workers prowled the outer aisles, keeping a close eye on the lanterns and the elongated canvas.

With impeccable timing, Reverend Inman stood up, and June felt the crowd's energy surge. Resolute voices became even more forceful with musical praise.

How did Reverend Inman accomplish such a miraculous transformation? Eli and Papa were mighty workers for the Lord. But Reverend Inman . . . Reverend Inman hummed with charisma—literally compelling the worshiper to follow God, to respond.

Tonight the offering baskets were passed again and again. June spotted Parker sitting toward the back. He was accompanied tonight by Simon and two other loggers. The big loggers filled the wooden bench. Parker looked over to catch June's eyes as the basket passed in front of him. She smiled, but his mouth tightened and accusation colored his features.

Disappointment swept over her. Parker had a powerful influence over his men. If he weren't so stubborn, so *thickheaded,* he would support, not hinder, her work— Eli's work—and more importantly, God's work. Bitterness over Eli's death still twisted Parker's opinion of Reverend Inman. She had to concede that perhaps Reverend Inman was caught up in his dream—at times to the point of obsession—but it was still a worthy dream.

Jesus, she breathed, closing her eyes, *touch Parker's heart. Soften it toward your work. Allow him to see that Reverend Inman is only doing your will; his dream is to provide a place that will demonstrate the glorious splendor of God, a place like no other where people can worship God. Open Parker's eyes so that Reverend Inman's dream can be realized. Let him be a help instead of a hindrance.*

⁓

"Well, well, God's little emissary! You're gettin' to be a pest." Anthony Riggings dropped a coin in June's tin cup, and the teasing light left his eyes. "Wish it could be more, girlie."

"God will stretch it, Anthony. Remember the two fish and five loaves of bread?"

"Thought it was two loaves of bread and five fish."

"Nope," she teased. "Two mackerel and five loaves of cracked wheat." She grinned good-naturedly at the burly, red-headed logger. "Haven't seen you in services all week!"

Anthony faked a bad cough. "Been laid up, I have."

"You'll be back soon?"

He coughed again, more convincingly this time. "Shore plan to try."

June grinned, shaking her head as he

wove down the street. She guessed she couldn't expect money *and* a miracle.

Dumping the coins into a bag, she buttoned her cloak and hurried to the waiting buggy. She'd promised to go to the tabernacle site with Reverend Inman this afternoon.

Visiting the site had turned into a daily ritual for him. Reverend Inman seemed to draw sustenance from the rite, as if seeing the land it would occupy, visualizing the tabernacle again and again, kept the vision alive in his mind.

"I can see it," Reverend Inman said, sweeping his hand parallel with the horizon as they stood at the site. "The auditorium will be there—so the morning sun will stream through the windows."

June knew the planned structure by heart. Reverend Inman would go on and on about building plans. Wooden stakes surrounded the construction area. Reverend Inman had staked the site with such joy, such adoration, it was exhilarating to watch.

"Come spring, ground will be broken," he promised. "We will build the tabernacle from lumber taken from these very woods

so the people will feel a part of it all." His
eyes burned with fevered conviction. "I've
patterned the tabernacle after a cathedral
Katherine and I once saw in England—
have I mentioned that? People will come
by land and by sea to witness this glorious spectacle." Arms spread wide, he obviously envisioned the wondrous sight.

"Across the front will be three sweeping
gables: one over the double front door
and one over each portal.

"Over the front door I see a rose-
colored window, a circle, representing
eternity. Flanking the window, two multifoil
windows over double lancet windows.
Stained glass, yes, beautiful stained glass.
When the sun streams through the colored
panes, the interior will be bathed in
heaven's light.

"Here—above the stained glass, I'll
build a cross erected between two towers." He clasped a balled fist to his
mouth, choked with emotion. "I wish—
how I wish the towers could be marble,
but the money—always the money."

Turning, his eyes reviewed the uneven
ground. "I'll place the altar here, seats for
the clergy and choir in the chancel. The

pulpit here." His gaze centered on the area where the front wall would stand.

"When the doors are thrown open, the altar will be in full view, the choir loft behind. Behind the choir I picture a pristine white wall with a wooden cross. The grain of the wood will imitate bloodstains."

June was momentarily disconcerted, frightened almost, by the reverend's intensity. His eyes burned with fanatical zeal. Reverend Inman's words became Eli's, or was it the other way around? Eli had used the same grand description when he visualized the shrine. She thought it was his dream too, but was it possible Reverend Inman had imagined the tabernacle aloud so many times that the words had become ingrained in Eli's mind?

When June left a short while later, she felt a sense of unease. Something troubled her. Something that remained, nagged, hung on the rest of the day.

After services that evening, June collected the baskets and took them into a small alcove behind the stage.

Reverend Inman swept into the small space as she finished, his features animated tonight.

"God moved among his people to-night!"

"Yes," June murmured absently, stacking coins into one-dollar piles.

Reverend Inman peered over her shoulder. "The offering doesn't look as generous as previous nights."

"It's most generous," she assured him.

He frowned as his eye skimmed the piles of coins. "No, no, I'm sure it isn't. Were all the baskets passed? If the offerings fall off, the tabernacle will suffer. We can't allow that to happen. God's people must be involved." He started to pace the cramped space, speaking to no one in particular. "It's imperative—the people must be a part of this great venture."

He paused, pinching his lower lip between his thumb and forefinger. "I must enhance the commitment. I must be more adamant about the tabernacle's significance."

June glanced up. There was something about his demeanor. Gone was the charismatic, commanding figure who had spoken so eloquently from the pulpit earlier, a man who knelt and prayed with the sick and the hurting. A man who, with tears

streaming down his cheeks, prayed with
the sinner for redemption. Now he spoke
as if the tabernacle were all consuming,
as if nothing else mattered.

Reverend Inman ceased pacing. "Tomorrow night I will preach on the man
who built bigger barns." Digging his
pocket watch out of his vest, he snapped
it open and noted the time. "It's late. Will
you be all right here alone?"

"Of course—"

"When you're finished, you will put the
offering into the safe and lock it. Do you
understand?"

"I understand." She followed the same
ritual every night. "Ben always helps me."

"Good. Ben's a good man. I'll go over
the ledgers in the morning."

When Reverend Inman left, June sat for
a moment, staring at the piles of coins
covering the scarred wooden table. So
much money—staggering amounts—and
yet Reverend Inman was distraught with
the shortfall. For the life of her, she
couldn't understand why. Was Reverend
Inman beginning to lose perspective?
She'd heard Papa talk about good men
who lost sight of their intent and became

caught up in their eagerness to achieve. She shook the troubling thought aside. She'd been in a strange mood all day. Why should she question Reverend Inman's motives? She had been so sure God had sought Reverend Inman out to build the tabernacle. Eli had been sure.

Funds must be raised to further God's kingdom, and that was her purpose now. She'd never heard Reverend Inman purposely ply guilt in order to spur healthier offerings.

She finished counting the money, entered the final tally into the ledger, and put it and the money into the safe. She turned the lock.

She jumped when Ben unexpectedly poked his head through the tent opening. "Do you need Ben, Miss June?"

Hand over her heart, June met his expectant gaze. "No, I've taken care of the money, Ben. You can go home."

Ben grinned. "Thank you." His childlike eyes scanned her dress. "You look so pretty tonight. I like blue."

Her cheeks grew hot at the compliment. "Thank you, Ben."

"Mr. Parker was here tonight?"

"Yes, he was here." She recalled the way Parker's eyes had turned on her in silent accusation during the offering. Did he attend services to be her accuser, or did he attend in order to worship his heavenly Father?

Reverend Inman's earlier mood clouded her mind as she slipped into her cloak. Parker clearly wanted no part of the tabernacle, yet he attended Reverend Inman's services. Did he honestly feel the tabernacle was an obsession for Reverend Inman—that Reverend Inman, without knowing it, was consumed with the project?

Had he seen in Reverend Inman something she had barely glimpsed tonight?

She blew out the lamp and let herself out. Waving good night to Ben, she walked toward the complex.

Parker must be wrong about Reverend Inman. The reverend was a man of God. His people adored him, and he loved them back. He would never compromise God's work to gratify his own desires.

Given enough time, she would prove Parker wrong—make him see that Reverend Inman's dream was God's plan.

Chapter Seven

June was dressing Saturday morning when a knock sounded at her door. She hurriedly fastened the last hook on her black wool dress. Who could be calling so early?

"Hey in there! Open up! You got yourself a visitor!"

"Sam!" June squealed with delight, nearly tipping over the vanity as she rushed to open the door.

"And who else could it be with a voice like this?" Samantha Harris challenged.

Flinging open the door, June threw herself into Sam's arms and hugged her. The two girls giggled and danced a half circle, holding each other. June finally stood back for a good look at her dear friend. "If you aren't a sight for sore eyes!"

Sam grinned, her big hazel eyes rich with mischief. "Look like somethin' the cats dragged in, ay?"

Laughing, June pulled her into the room and closed the door. "What do you think of the complex?"

"Interesting, lovey—a bit confusin' to live in, is it not?"

Squeezing Sam's hand affectionately, June drank in the sight of her. She hadn't realized until this moment how very much she missed her. "It's so good to see you."

"It's good to see you too, lovey! Sorry it took so long." Her freckled features sobered. "I've been wantin' to come see you, desperately so, I 'ave. But me Aunt Angie . . . well, she's been quite ill these days, taken to her bed, she 'as."

June wanted to console her. "I'm so sorry. Is there anything I can do?"

"No . . . not much anyone can do," Sam admitted.

June drew her back into her arms for another close embrace. "Oh, Sam! God can! Tonight I'll request special prayer for her at services."

Sam brightened. "Would you, lovey? I'd be most appreciative!"

"I'd pray regardless, but don't you worry. God can have your aunt feeling better in no time." Draping her arm around Sam's boyish shoulders, June steered her to the only chair in the room.

Sam glanced around the small quarters, grinning. "Got yourself a quaint little place here."

Regardless of the size of her new home, June was grateful for the shelter it provided. The complex was old and drafty, and Ettie was forever saying Reverend Inman desperately needed to build a new one—but, of course, that would take money, money the ministry didn't have. "I'm comfortable here, truly I am. And everyone is so good to me."

Sam elbowed her with a knowing wink. "Suppose that includes 'ubby! I'll wager all of London 'e's not complainin'. Considers it to be quite the cozy place for 'imself and 'is smashing new bride."

June's face fell. In all the excitement she'd forgotten about Eli. "No . . . Eli isn't complaining. Didn't you get my message?"

"Message?" Sam tilted her head, a sly grin on her face. "Are you pullin' me leg? I didn't get any message." Her features suddenly sobered. "Is somethin' amiss?"

"Sam . . . my husband-to-be—Eli Messenger—passed away before we could be married."

For a moment the words didn't appear to have registered. Then Sam's hand shot to her heart, and the color drained from under her freckles. "Passed away? As in . . . died?"

June sank to the side of the bed. Poor Sam, the news must have come as a shock. She'd paid a messenger one nickel to go to the orphanage and inform Sam about Eli's death, but apparently the scallywag had fled with the money. It was still difficult for her to think about Eli's untimely death, much less talk about it. She reached for a hankie on the nightstand.

Sam knelt by the bedside to console her. "Come on, now. 'e isn't really dead, a young man like 'im. You can be honest with me, lovey."

June shook her head. "He's gone, Sam."

"Well, 'ow dare 'e!" Sam stood up, ready to fight. Her eyes scanned the tiny quarters. "Now where did the rogue run off to? Never you worry, lovey, 'e'll not get away with breakin' your 'eart. We'll hunt 'im down like a dog, we will, and when we find the scoundrel we'll—"

June took a deep breath and interrupted her tirade. "Eli is dead, Sam. When I arrived, Eli was very sick. Remember? Reverend Inman met us at the dock? Everyone thought Eli was getting better. We barely had time to introduce ourselves before . . . well, before the Lord called him home."

Sam whistled under her breath. "Oh, dear. Then 'e is . . ."

June nodded. "Dead."

"Oh my . . . how awful. So sorry, lovey. What a bloomin' rotten turn of luck."

"I'm trying not to question what's happened. God called Eli home. I don't understand why, but I know there must be a reason."

Nodding, Sam blew her nose, which

was suddenly red with emotion. "Aye, me auntie says there's just some things we aren't supposed to question." She was silent for a long moment. "Still, it's a bloomin' shame. Just a bloomin' shame."

June nodded. "A bloomin' shame." Once the tabernacle was built, she would feel obligated to return to Cold Water.

Sam sat down at the table, toying with June's hairbrush. "So, what will you do now?"

"I'm going to stay on and finish the work Eli started."

Sam looked up expectantly. "And what work is that, lovey?"

June explained the tabernacle and how Eli and Reverend Inman shared the same dream. There was so much she wanted to tell Sam, so many hopes, so many fears. "I've collected over two hundred dollars in the short time I've been here."

"Ow, now that's lovely. It's like me mum says. There's nothin' a woman can't do if she sets 'er mind to it."

June dried her tears, hope overtaking her pessimism. If God had a purpose for her, he would sustain her. Leaning across the table, she clasped Sam's freckled hand. "We have so much to talk about. Can you stay the afternoon?"

"Yes, today is one of Auntie's better days. I needn't be back till time for evenin' chores."

"Wonderful! Are you hungry? Would you like to go for a walk? I'll ask Ettie to bring—"

"Whoa, whoa! I'm not 'ungry." She patted her flat stomach. "Gettin' fat as a hog, I am. All those beans and potatoes. A nice, brisk walk would do me heart good!"

Elated to be reunited, June happily agreed. A day with her best friend was exactly what she needed.

On the way out, the women stopped by the kitchen and pilfered two large buttermilk biscuits, generously spread with Ettie's blackberry jam. In between sticky bites, they giggled and caught up on the news.

"Has your Aunt Angie been sick long?"

"Aye, but she's worsened over the month. Some days are better than others. To look at 'er you'd think there was nothing amiss." Sam licked blackberry jam from between her fingers. "Doc says it's 'er 'eart. Plumb worn to a nubbin, it is. I'm not surprised. She's given a 'unk of it to everyone who's ever needed it. And she is gettin' on in years, you know."

"How old is she?"

"She says seventy-three, but I think it's more like eighty." She took a bite of biscuit, chewing thoughtfully. "Me mum says it's only a matter of time. Can't bear the thought of losing me auntie, but it's the children's plight that pains me more."

"The orphans?"

"Aye, the poor wee tykes. Don't know what will happen to them when Auntie passes on. She takes in stray kiddies like some folks take in abandoned kitties."

June was afraid she knew the answer. Cold Water had a small orphanage. It was run down and needy, managed by an elderly couple who loved children. When Edward Rugby died and then a year later his wife, Millie, passed away, the poor babies were left with no one to look after them. If Aunt Angeline died, her orphans would undoubtedly be fated to be uprooted again. "What will happen to the children?"

Sam's face firmed. "They'll stay together, if I have me say about it."

"You? Sam, you can't possibly take on such a responsibility by yourself. How old are you?"

"Seventeen, come next winter."

Barely sixteen, and this girl with a heart of gold was willing to give her life in service to the orphanage. Sam stiffened with pride. "I can do it, I can! Sick as Auntie's been, she barely pulls 'er share of the load now. Taught me a thing or two, she has. Besides, I got Ol' Joe." She grinned. "And even though Joe might be pushing eighty, he ain't goin' nowhere. Leastways, not anytime soon. He's fit as a fiddle and strong as an ox."

"Ol' Joe who?"

"Ol' Joe—the Indian man. You remember—he came to fetch me the day we got here."

June did recall an elderly white-haired gentleman standing beside a wagon with *Angeline's Orphanage* painted on the sides.

"Sam—is he dangerous?"

"Dangerous?" Sam had a good laugh. "Ol' Joe? 'e's about the nicest Yakima you'd ever want to meet."

June paled. "What's a Yakima?"

Sam laughed all the harder. "You're a bloomin' innocent! Yakima is a native tribe that live in these parts."

"Where did Aunt Angie get Ol' Joe?"

"Where did she get him? Ain't like she fetched 'im from the mercantile along with the rest of the supplies."

June felt incredibly foolish. "Of course not. I just meant—"

"Ow, I know what you meant, lovey. No matter. Ol' Joe just showed up on Auntie's doorstep one day, cold, hungry, nowhere left to go after the war."

"War?"

"The war—you know, the nasty dispute the settlers had with the Yakima a long time ago."

June was impressed with Sam's knowledge of the area's heritage. She didn't know a thing about any war.

"Joe was much younger then. 'Course Aunt Angie was too. 'e needed work, and Aunt Angie sure needed 'elp, so she took 'im in and 'e's lived there ever since. Been a real godsend, 'e 'as."

"If an Indian ever showed up on my doorstep, I would be scared to death," June confessed. "Here's one of my favorite places." She stopped at the edge of a small pond.

Sam rolled her eyes. "Ya big scaredy. It was a bit spooky at first. Neither Auntie nor Joe could speak each other's language. And their customs were so different from each other's. They must have made quite a sight."

June smiled, picturing the colorful aunt and the Yakima. "But it all worked out?"

"This is a beautiful place, June." Sam leaned over and picked up a rock to skip across the pond. The water shimmered like glass in the bright sunshine. "Worked out quite well, actually. First they taught each other their native language, which, according to Auntie, was no easy task. But I suppose the most difficult part was adapting to each other's customs. Auntie Angie reads the Bible every night. As soon as Ol' Joe could understand the words, 'e couldn't get enough. 'e used to be called by his Yakima name. Auntie thought it proper he be given a Christian name. She settled on Job. Joe liked that, liked it real well. But it didn't take long to see it wasn't fittin'.

"Joe didn't have a whole lot of patience; still doesn't. So, on one of 'is particularly testy days, Auntie jerked the Job off, and she's called 'im Joe ever since."

June laughed, recalling how Aunt Thalia lacked patience too. "Did Joe make her smoke a peace pipe?"

"Ol' Joe? He'd been choked if 'e'd dared to try, but Auntie did make 'im do the dishes. Took 'im forever to get the knack of it. 'ates it, 'e does. Been tryin' to get out of it ever since!"

June sighed. "I don't know, Sam. It all sounds so scary to me."

Sam paused to look at her. "Joe doin' the dishes?" She giggled. "Nothin' scary 'bout it, lovey. Joe teases that 'e's the only Yakima in these parts with dishpan hands!"

"No, no, Ol' Joe doesn't sound scary; it's scary that your aunt is ill and the children will have no one if something should happen to her."

"Aye, that part is scary, it is. They'll have Joe and me, but we won't be able to do much to 'old it together. Auntie's barely able to keep food on the table and shoes on the kiddies' feet."

"You're sure Ol' Joe is harmless?" June kidded.

Sam solemnly crossed her heart. "Honest Injun!"

Both burst into laughter. June was relieved to lighten the mood.

"Seriously," Sam said with great certainty, "Joe's real good about helping. Chauffeurs Auntie and the children anywhere they need to go. Tends the garden, chops wood, hauls water. Whatever needs doin', he's right there. I don't even think of him as an Indian, a Brit, or a Yank, for that matter. He's just a decent man."

June agreed. Yakima, white, or any color of the rainbow, he was one of God's children. He need be nothing more, and certainly he was nothing less. She stood. "Come on. I have something I want you to see."

The two young women walked across the meadow and turned to climb a small rise.

"Where are we goin'?" Sam bent over and rubbed the backs of her legs. "Me dogs are killin' me."

"Your dogs?" June glanced behind her. She hadn't seen any dogs.

Sam lifted a heavy boot and pointed. "Dogs."

"Oh, your feet!" June laughed. "Well, let's shed these boots."

Sam didn't need a second invitation. She dropped to the ground and stripped off the heavy leather boots. Her feet were generously sprinkled with the same russet freckles as her face.

June quickly joined her, and soon they were both barefoot, wiggling their toes with newfound freedom. Tying their boot strings together, they slung the shoes across their shoulders and started up the grassy embankment. It was far too cold to be going barefoot; the abrasive blades of grass were like icy needles beneath their toes.

"Isn't this the grandest thing!" Sam wiggled her freckled toes in ankle-tall weeds.

"It's marvelous!" June felt lighthearted and carefree for the first time in weeks. Aunt Thalia would have apoplexy if she knew June was going barefoot this soon.

"You never did say where we are 'eading."

"You'll see." June wanted to surprise

her. "I'm taking you to a special place
that will suck the breath right out of you.
A sight unlike any you've ever seen!"

Sam eyed her curiously. "I'm not terribly
sure I want to 'ave the breath sucked out
of me."

June laughed. It was wonderful to feel
young again! "Look, Sam! Another pond.
This one has cattails!"

"Cat's what?"

"Cattails—come on. Let's pick some!"

"Have you lost your bloomin' mind!
What would we do with a bouquet of animal tails!" Sam protested as June pulled
her toward the water's edge.

"You'll see!"

The girls busied themselves picking cattails, arranging them in a huge brown bouquet.

Sam waded out of the water and
handed hers to June. "Here, lovey. I think
you've lost your bloomin' mind."

Smiling, June took her hand, and the
two girls raced back to the rise. When
they reached the top, they paused to
catch their breath. June pointed below. A
single white cross stood alone in the
peaceful meadow.

"They're for Eli. I try to bring fresh ones whenever I can."

"Oh, lovey—" Sam took her hand—"I'm sorry."

"You needn't be." June smiled. "Eli's in a far better place. I bring the cattails to remind passersby what a wonderful person he was."

Sam frowned. "Shouldn't you be bringing flowers?"

June gave her a pained look. "Sam, where would I find flowers this time of year in Seattle?"

"I say, I quite forgot for a moment where we were. Cattails are just fine."

The two women placed the bouquet on the mound of fresh dirt beneath the white cross. For a moment they stood in silence, paying their respects to Eli Messenger, a young man buried beneath a simple cross with a crudely engraved marker that read, "Asleep in Jesus."

June's hand crept into Sam's. "He would have been a very good husband."

"Aye, that 'e would, lovey. The best."

Halfway across the meadow, the ground sloped to a tranquil valley. The view was mesmerizing. Tall pines stretched into the flawless blue sky. The spicy scent of pine perfumed the air.

"Wow!" Sam murmured. "Do you suppose heaven must look a bit like this?"

June glowed. "Do you like it?"

Sam's eyes welled with appreciation. "Like it? It's so lovely it makes me puddle."

"Not a prettier place this side of heaven."

"I bloomin' well reckon not!" Sam sniffed, wiping her eyes with the sleeves of her dress.

"This is where Reverend Inman plans to build the tabernacle."

"Clean down there!" Sam exclaimed. "He must be off his nut! How will he ever—?"

June laughed. "Not down there. Up here. Right here—on the very spot where we're standing."

"I'm not one to know much about such matters," Sam admitted. Her freckles stood out in the harsh, cold light. She glanced around uneasily. "Should we be standing on such sacred ground?"

Nodding, June took a deep breath of the sweet air. "We're God's children. We can stand on any ground we want, 'cause we're heirs to the kingdom!'' she proclaimed proudly.

"That's so beautiful, it makes me want to pray," Sam said solemnly. "And that's something I don't do a whole lot of."

"Shame on you, Sam Harris." June took her hand and pulled her to her knees. "We'll pray together, right here, right now."

Sam groaned as her knees met the grassy knoll. June looked over at her solemnly. "Do you want to start?"

Sam shook her head.

"Then I will. Bow your head."

"Me toes are cold," Sam murmured. "Bloomin' well should have stayed 'ome today."

"Father, we bow before you, thanking you for this marvelous day, for shared friendship, for unspeakable beauty. We thank you for Eli Messenger's life, and for his death, for we know you can work both for your glory. Bless Reverend Inman; grant him wisdom and strength to bring hope to the hundreds of lost and lonely who gather every night to hear your Word.

"Forgive us our sins, and protect us

from harm. Bless Aunt Angie, and allow
her to remain with us a while longer, Lord.
She's needed so very much. Bless the
children, Lord. Keep them safe and happy
and protected. Bless Ol' Joe, and keep
him healthy so he can serve the children.

"Most of all, we praise you for your
love, for sending your only Son to die on
the cross so that we may have eternal life.
Forgive our sins, and help us to do better.
We ask in Jesus' name. Amen."

Pulling Sam to her feet, June smiled.
"Now, that wasn't so hard, was it?"

Sam rubbed her aching knees. "Not as
long as you do the talkin'. Do you come
here every day?"

"Every day. Come, let me show you the
tabernacle."

"Show me? It ain't been built yet, 'as
it?"

"No, but I can make you see it."

Sam listened intently as June described
the temple, its beauty and opulence, how
Reverend Inman planned to pattern it after
a great European cathedral, with the three
magnificent arches, the stately portals, the
beautiful stained-glass windows.

"It will surely cost a bloomin' fortune to build something like that!" Sam said.

"I suppose it will, but Reverend Inman says the Lord deserves the best."

"That's exactly what 'e'll be getting when this tabernacle is finished." Sam looked off in the distance, trouble coloring her features.

"Is something wrong?" June asked. She had detected a tone of sadness in Sam's voice.

"No, not really." Sam sat down, wiggling her toes. "It's bloomin' cold, it is."

"Want to put your boots on?"

"Not yet."

"Then what's wrong? Does something about the tabernacle bother you?"

"No—it's just all that money. When I think about what that amount of money, or just a smidgen of it, could do for the orphanage. . . . It could buy new shoes, schoolbooks, a woodstove for the upstairs. We 'ave a small one downstairs, but it can't begin to heat the entire house. And clothes. Nice warm coats and mittens. Clothes at the orphanage 'ave been 'anded down from one to the other so often that they're threadbare and hardly serviceable. Doesn't take long to go through clothes with all those kids—and more comin' every day. They come in all shapes and sizes, you know. From the oldest, twelve, right down to the toddler, who turned two last week."

June knew it must be difficult to feed and clothe so many children. "Others help, don't they? Donate money and food?"

Sam shook her head. "Aye, you'd think they would, and Auntie says they used to 'elp a sight more than they do now. The loggers are kind to the little ones, but nobody gives as much as they used to." She tsked. "There are so many in the community who could help. . . . Such a bloomin' shame."

"I know it must be difficult." Raising money for the tabernacle was hard enough. "Is there anything I can do to help?"

"Oh, lovey! Do you mean it? We can always use help!" Sam exclaimed.

"Then consider me an extra pair of hands. I have lots of free time, and I'd be more than glad to help. I haven't any money to offer, but I have a heart full of love, and Aunt Thalia says I can take a stove apart and black it as good as anybody. I can mop floors and hang wash. Not to be prideful, but you should taste my elderberry jelly. Papa said there was none better!"

"God bless you, June Kallahan! Not only can we use your help, but it will allow you and me to spend more time together. You'll love Auntie and the kids."

"I'd love to help, but I'll need to consult Reverend Inman. Then I'll need to re-arrange my schedule—perhaps I can spend mornings at the orphanage, after-noons in front of The Gilded Hen, and evenings at tent services counting the nightly offering. I have to keep my previ-ous commitments, but I think I should be able to help you out too."

Excitement welled in June. She would love the children. And it wouldn't interfere with her work for Reverend Inman or the tabernacle. She'd make sure of it. *Glory be! Praise God and alleluia!*

"I can't wait to get started!"

"When can you start?"

"Soon, Sam. I can't say exactly when—but soon."

Sam's face fell. "Ow. I was rather gettin' me 'opes up you could start tomorrow."

June shook her head. "Tomorrow is Sunday, Sam."

"Ow, yes—I suppose you'll be wanting to attend services."

"Not attend, teach."

Sam frowned. "Aye, now you be pullin' me leg."

"Sam, I would never pull your leg. I'm serious." June explained her plan to hold Sunday services at nearby logging camps, starting with Pine Ridge, Parker Sentell's camp.

"Well, that does sound admirable." Sam thought for a moment. "Who's Parker Sentell?"

Taking her arm, June turned her around, and they started back. A cold wind had sprung up, and clouds were rolling in. "Now that's a story that will take more than an afternoon to tell."

"Ow." Sam winked. "A right 'andsome one, ay?"

"Most handsome," June conceded. "And incredibly stubborn!"

"How on earth did you get those loggers to agree to church services? 'ear tell, they're real rascals.''

The observation reminded June of the day she had disregarded Parker's warning and gone into the rival camp alone. She shuddered. The men were rascals all right. Depraved ones. She didn't know what would have happened if Parker hadn't rescued her. June suddenly stopped, bringing her hands to her hips as she fixed Sam with a stern look. "Would you like to attend Sunday's service?"

"Ow, no, lovey. . . ." Sam looked doubtful.

"Wonderful!" June slipped her arm back through Sam's. "And someday very soon, you can take me to meet Aunt Angie and the children. Meanwhile, you can start coming to services. It will do you good."

"Ow dear, I've fell in it now, 'aven't I? Well . . . OK, I'll come to your services when I can—because you're such a good friend." Her eyes swept the darkening sky. "And if we've got a pound of smarts between us, I say we be 'eadin' back. From the looks of those clouds movin' in, we're apt to get caught in the middle of a gully washer."

June studied the bank of dark rain clouds. "I think you're right. And I think we'd best be putting our boots back on—in case we have to make a run for it."

"Or a swim for it," Sam groused.

The two women sat down on the grass and laced up their boots. When the last knot was tied, Sam sprang to her feet. "Race ya!"

In no time at all, Sam was little more than a speck in the distance. June was just getting to her feet.

When June reached the revival tent, a rested-looking Sam was perched jauntily on a bench, eating an apple. "Where you been, slowpoke?"

Trying to catch her breath, June leaned forward, panting. "Are you part rabbit?"

"Lynx," Sam conceded.

Exhausted, June dropped to the bench and tried to catch her breath. "I'm so glad you're here, Sam."

"Me too, lovey. Me too." Sam lifted her eyes to the threatening weather. "But I best be going. It's about to open up and pour any minute."

"I'll ask Ben to drive you home in the buggy."

"Nah, I got Sissy." Sam pitched the apple core away, then brushed dust from her skirt.

"Sissy?"

"Me mule." Pulling June to her feet, she propelled her to the side of the tent, where she'd tied the animal earlier. "Meet Sissy, one fine mule."

"But you'll get soaked!" June protested as she felt the first sprinkling of raindrops hit her cheek.

"Not me." Sam bunched up her skirt and slid bareback onto the mule.

"You will unless you've got feathers like a duck!"

"Got me something even better." Sam reached across Sissy's bridle and prominently displayed her treasure. "I got me a bumbershoot."

Sissy turned her head, staring at June with big brown eyes that would melt a stone.

With a flick of her wrist, Sam proudly snapped the faded red umbrella open.

The sudden noise made June jump. She doubted anything so tattered would protect Sam from a sprinkle, let alone a downpour. The umbrella was so small, it scarcely covered Sam's head.

"Are you sure you don't want Ben to drive you? It'd be no trouble."

Sam gently nudged Sissy's flanks. "See you tomorrow then . . . at services. Pine Ridge, you say?"

"Nine o'clock."

"Nine o'clock."

"Sharp."

"Sharp."

The big gray mule obediently trotted off. "See you tomorrow!" Sam waved with her left hand, holding the reins and umbrella in her right, bouncing high on Sissy's back.

An hour after revival services, people still milled around the tent. The altar call had lasted unusually long; fifty or more had come to profess their faith. June had a difficult time keeping her mind on business. Hard as she tried, she kept seeing Sam on the back of that old mule, waving that silly "bumbershoot." She prayed that her friend had made it safely back to the orphanage and that Aunt Angie wasn't any worse. . . . If anything happened to Aunt

Angie, the orphans would have to find new homes. . . . They had worn-out shoes—improper heating. They needed so much.

When the tent eventually cleared, June disappeared into the small room behind the pulpit to count money. Ben and several other ushers piled the overflowing collection baskets on the large wooden table. Tonight's service was large and required that even more baskets be passed. The offerings seemed endless.

Counting the donations, June's mind returned to the orphans. Sam's words about the needs at the orphanage turned over in her mind. Shoes, clothes, food.

June shook the troubling thoughts aside. The tabernacle was important too. The orphanage served the needs of a pitiful few. The tabernacle would serve thousands.

The kerosene lamp burned low when she finally finished. She penciled the amount in the ledger, tucking it and the money inside the safe.

Pulling on her cloak, she thought of the orphans again. New shoes, warm clothes, adequate food, a stove for upstairs.

Hardly selfish needs—important ones, that desperately needed to be addressed.

Her gaze focused on the safe. The outpouring of love had been so large tonight. Perhaps if she were to bring the children's needs to Reverend Inman's attention, he would help. Just a portion—perhaps twenty dollars? The amount would purchase staples for the orphanage for a month, if nothing else.

As she was about to snuff out the lamp and go in search of the reverend, he suddenly pulled back the curtain and entered the room.

"Reverend."

"Hello, my dear. Wonderful service tonight—so many responses. The angels surely are rejoicing."

Reverend Inman removed his wire-rimmed glasses and polished them with his handkerchief. June noticed that his worn overcoat had seen better days.

"Reverend, you should buy yourself a new coat. The one you're wearing isn't adequate protection against the cold wind."

"Nonsense. It's fine—any spare coin I have goes toward the tabernacle." He rubbed his hands together to warm them. "Did you see the crowd tonight? Did you see how they came to hear God's Word, to receive his blessings? Praise God!"

"Oh, yes, Reverend Inman, I saw." June's eyes focused on the safe. So many needs. Warm clothes, adequate food, a stove for the upstairs.

"God's been good to his people."

"Very good."

The reverend hooked his glasses over his ears, then looked around. "You're awfully quiet tonight. Have a big day?"

"Yes. . . . Reverend, I'd like to speak to you about a personal matter."

His eyes softened with concern. "Of course—please, say whatever's in your heart."

"You know the small orphanage on the outskirts of Seattle?"

"Oh, yes. Angeline's. Wonderful woman doing an admirable job with those children."

"My friend Sam—Samantha Harris—you remember Sam? She was with me the day you met me at the dock."

"Yes, I remember Sam. A bright child, freckle faced and precocious."

June grinned. "That's Sam."

"What about her? Does she need special prayer?"

"That would be nice, Reverend, but Sam's not the problem; it's her Aunt Angeline. She cares for the orphans, and she's very ill."

"Yes, you requested prayer for Angeline this evening. I'm sure the Lord will hear her needs."

"Yes, I believe he will." June paused. "But the orphanage has dire needs right now, needs that have to be addressed."

"Did you pray for those needs to be met?"

June glanced at the safe. "I prayed, Reverend, and I'm hoping we can do more than pray. I thought perhaps the ministry might be willing to give the orphanage a small donation. The children need shoes and warm clothing. There's only one stove in the drafty house, and they desperately need a second stove for the upstairs bedrooms. If the crusade could share even a small portion of tonight's offering for the children—not a lot, maybe twenty dollars. Just enough to help—"

She faltered when Reverend Inman shook his head sadly.

"I'm afraid that would be out of the question. The crusade money is for the tabernacle."

"Yes, I know. But twenty dollars—the money would hardly be missed."

Reverend Inman shook his head again. "My heart goes out to the children, and I deeply wish the ministry could be of assistance, but there are so many needs, and so few funds to meet them. No, we cannot use tabernacle funds for other purposes."

June's spirit sagged.

The reverend's features gentled. "I understand your concern, June dear, but we must keep our focus on the tabernacle. God's work must be our first priority. The tabernacle will portray his glory to all who see it. Glory be to God."

June wanted to help the orphans as well as see the tabernacle built. Both were worthy causes.

"But twenty dollars, Reverend. The people give so generously—all they can spare."

Patting her shoulder, the reverend busied himself reading the night's tally. Obviously he considered the matter closed.

June sighed. She'd lost this battle. She was a mere lamb, and Reverend Inman was the shepherd. He was wiser than she, and he knew the most urgent need. He would never lead his followers astray. . . .

Her heart was heavy as she let herself out of the tent a few minutes later and closed the flap behind her. Reverend Inman had promised to extinguish the lamp.

The children needed warm clothes, shoes, proper food. The concern refused to leave her.

Twenty dollars was a lot—but so little to ask for the orphans' sake.

Perhaps if she mentioned the orphans' needs to Parker tomorrow, he would allow her to. . . .

No, he'd forbidden her to take up an offering. She could hold services, but she wasn't allowed to accept donations.

When she blew out the light and climbed into bed a short while later, her mind was still on the orphans. Clothes. Nourishing food. A second stove to warm a cold bedroom floor.

Rolling onto her back, she stared at the ceiling.

Souls saved. God's Word proclaimed to thousands. The tabernacle.

Which was the more worthy need?

Chapter Eight

Pigs! June had never seen so many pigs! White pigs, black pigs, big pigs, little pigs, white sows with their litters beside them, all rooting beneath the pines for acorns.

June shook her head at the comical sight. Pine Ridge Logging Camp was alive with pigs!

"Did ya ever see so many 'ogs in your life?" Sam sat up straighter, straining to get a better look. "Does Mr. Sentell raise 'ogs or cut timber?"

June frowned. "Apparently a little of both."

Sam tucked a lock of windblown hair beneath her bonnet as June drove the buckboard through an open gate. "There won't be none of that carryin' on and prayin' out loud, will there now, lovey?"

June swerved the buggy to avoid a boar sprawled sideways in the middle of the road. "Some—but I won't call on you to pray aloud."

"Right ducky of you," Sam grumbled. "Don't know 'ow I let meself get talked into this."

June made a face at her. "Samantha Harris, the Lord loves you despite your heathenish attitude." Sam needed a little spiritual tune-up, and June happily accepted the challenge.

The wind was nippy this morning in spite of a dazzling blue sky overhead. June welcomed the change to dry weather. Above, geese flew in a pretty, symmetrical formation. June concentrated on the message she wanted to bring to the women.

"I'll be speaking on faithfulness this morning."

Sam's mouth dropped open. "Be steppin' on a few toes, I'll wager."

"I'll do my best to avoid yours." June patted Sam's head and laughed.

The logging camp was active for Sunday morning. June frowned when she recalled that Parker hadn't attended a single crusade service this week. Where had he been? Eli had said Parker wasn't married, but she wondered if perhaps a woman occupied his thoughts. The idea intrigued her. That might explain his odd conduct, his lack of patience, his downright boorish behavior at times. Of course at other times, he could be very nice.

She was surprised when her thoughts took off in a new direction. Exactly what sort of woman would interest the gruff, opinionated logger—perhaps one of the scantily dressed women employed at The Gilded Hen? The notion left her feeling unsettled, though she couldn't imagine why.

Simon met the wagon as it rolled to a stop in front of the camp office. A shy grin spread across the giant's rugged features as he extended a hand to help June down.

"Good morning, Miss Kallahan. I've been expecting you."

"Good morning, Simon." June gave him a warm smile as she removed her gloves.

It was interesting how Simon's gaze fixed solidly on Sam.

June glanced at Sam. It was clear to see she had no objections to the intense perusal.

"Simon, this is my friend, Samantha Harris. Sam is helping with services this morning."

Smiling, Simon effortlessly lifted Sam out of the buggy and set her lightly on her feet. The two continued to stare at each other as if this were their first encounter with the opposite sex.

Clearing her throat, June brought the moment back to the business at hand. "Simon, there's a box of study material in the bed of the wagon. If you would be so kind as to carry it in for me?"

"Yes, ma'am." Simon's eyes remained riveted on Sam's.

"Simon?"

He glanced up. "Yes, ma'am?"

"Please, don't call me ma'am." That made her sound like an old woman. "June will be fine."

"Yes, ma'am—June." Simon reached for the box of study material and hefted it onto his wide shoulder. A sea of ridged muscles played in his forearms. June hid a smile when Sam gaped at the display of brawny masculinity.

June fell in step with Simon, aware of the curious eyes now focused in their direction.

Men paused in front of sudsy washtubs, watching the entourage as they moved through camp. Others were playing cards on a nearby porch. Two men in barber chairs lay back in the warm sunshine and enjoyed a shave.

"Don't mind all the gawking," Simon called over his shoulder. "We don't get many women up this way."

"But you have some?" June questioned. Otherwise, her purpose to hold camp services would be useless. Surely Parker would have said if there were no women in camp! Her footsteps momentarily slowed. She started to fume. She wouldn't put it past him to let her come all the way up here for nothing.

"Well?" she prodded.

"Oh, there are a few," Simon conceded. "Eddy Crager's wife, Mary. She's a cook. Loren Jacobs's and Jim Bushy's families live up here, though Ellen Bushy doesn't

like it. Come spring, she'll be leaving.
Can't take the isolation anymore."

Sam turned to peer over her shoulder at
the activity. "Why are the men washing
their clothes on Sunday?"

Simon flashed her a friendly grin. "Sunday's boil-up day—the day the men de-
louse their blankets and clothing."

"Sunday's the Lord's day." June wrin-
kled her nose at the peculiar tang that
saturated the air. "What's that smell?"

"Laundry soap, scalding water, and
Peerless tobacco. It's the only thing we've
found to kill lice."

June shuddered. "Lice."

"Yes, ma'am." His features sobered.
"We try real hard to get rid of them." Simon headed for the cookshack. "Parker
said for you to hold services in here. We
eat dinner at eleven on Sundays. You'll
need to be through by then."

They entered the cookshack, and June
deeply inhaled the pleasant aroma of
fresh-baked cinnamon rolls.

Setting the box on the table, Simon
looked at Sam. "I have a few things left to
attend to. I'll be back for the services."

Sam flushed a pretty red.

The door closed behind him, and June laughed. "I think he likes you."

"Ow, what a crock of rubbish. The bloke barely knows me."

"Still—" June stripped off her bonnet— "by the gleam in his eyes, I think he'd like to know you better."

A few minutes before nine, Mary Crager removed her apron, hooked it over the back of a chair, and took her seat at the long table. June welcomed her with a friendly smile.

"Mary?"

The woman nodded. She was painfully thin, with shoulder-length brown hair that could stand a good washing. June recognized shyness in her doleful nut brown eyes. Her hands were rough and reddened from hard work and scalding dishwater. In her right one, she clutched a small, worn Bible.

"I'm glad you could come," June said, and meant it. She hadn't known how many to expect in the first service. One was a promising start.

Sam fished in the box and handed Mary a colorful chain of Bible verses. "Here, lovey. June made 'em herself, she did."

Mary's smile was saintly as she modestly accepted the gift. "Thank you. . . . I've . . . looked forward to you coming all week."

"God bless you," June said softly.

The door opened, and two women entered. Ellen Bushy and Amy Jacobs walked to the table and sat down at the end of the bench, their eyes darting around the room. They clearly were uncomfortable with the situation.

Sam forced a paper chain on them, though they protested, each trying to give Sam a coin in return.

"It's free, lovey. June made 'em."

The women perused the paper chains, exchanging dubious looks.

"It's all right," June explained. "They're Bible verses. You can refer to them during the coming week."

The women slowly nodded as if that was acceptable.

By ten minutes after nine, Simon and two men who introduced themselves as Pete Ridges and Arnold Atkinson joined the service. June stood up, her gaze encompassing her small flock, and her heart swelled with joy. She expected the services to be small; size didn't matter. Where two or more gathered in his name, God promised to be there also.

She glanced up expectantly as the door opened again, hoping Parker had decided to attend. Instead she saw a burly logger carrying a fifty-pound sack of potatoes on his shoulder. He walked past the bench and strode back to the kitchen.

Opening her Bible, June sighed, ignoring a prick of disappointment. She glanced up when the door opened again, and this time her hopes were realized. Her heart thumped when she saw Parker standing at the back of the room, arms crossed, waiting for services to begin. For the life of her, she didn't know why his approval should matter to her. But oddly enough, it did.

Releasing a pent-up breath she hadn't realized she was holding, she reminded herself that at least he was here. That was more than she'd expected.

Smiling, she welcomed the small group. All in all, the services were off to a promising start.

A month later Parker stood at his office window, arms akimbo, watching Simon load a box into June's buggy after the morning worship service. Services were going better than he had expected, but he still thought he was going to live to regret allowing her into camp. If he got wind she was attempting to raise funds for Inman, she would be gone before she could say, "God bless you."

Guilt nagged at him for not participating in the services. He attended because Sunday was the Lord's Day and up until now worship opportunities had been pretty slim. But wild horses couldn't make him tell her he actually approved of her interference. From the time he'd been knee-high to a grasshopper, he'd attended church services. Uncle Walt had insisted on it; Aunt Lacey upheld the edict with a stiff hickory switch. Stubbornness was the only thing keeping him from actually taking part in Miss-High-and-Mighty Kallahan's service.

The memory of Uncle Walt sobered him. Where had Walt gone wrong?

June must think I'm a cold, cantankerous man, Parker mused. She couldn't be

more wrong. . . . Not that it bothered him
a bit what her opinion of him was. He was
a thinking man. And he happened to *think*
Isaac Inman, just like Uncle Walt, had let
his desire to serve the Lord get out of
hand.

Building that fancy tabernacle, using
money to construct an extravagant exhibition that would bring thousands of strangers streaming into the area to view the
spectacle! Thousands of people would be
crowding the streets, overflowing the ho-
tels, making a nuisance of themselves.
The church itself would be miles from the
logging camps, but it would still interfere
with everything.

He rubbed the back of his neck. Why
would he care what June Kallahan or anybody else thought of him?

He glanced out the window again. Why
was he so restless today? His eyes focused on the gentle sway of June's skirt
as she climbed into the wagon, chatting
with Simon and Sam. Deep down he knew
why. He wasn't able to get those orphans
out of his mind.

The community did little anymore to
help their plight; and for the past year, he

and his men hadn't been able to keep up
with the necessities. A few baskets of groceries here and there, a few monetary donations. It wasn't enough. The children's
needs were not even close to being met.

"Mr. Sentell."

Parker looked up to see one of his men
standing in the doorway. "Hello, Chester.
What can I do for you?"

Chester King was a tall, lanky man. He
was one of Parker's oldest employees, as
well as one of his most trusted.

Chester paused in the doorway, red
faced. "I hate to ask, Mr. Sentell. But I
was wonderin' if I might be able to get a
draw on my pay. Just a small one. I
wouldn't ask, but the wife's mother came
down sick, and my Betta needs to go to
Portland to look after her. I know payday's
still a ways away—"

Parker opened the desk drawer and
took out the cash box. "How much do
you need, Chester?"

"Just enough for a stage ticket. I figure
payday will roll around before Betta's ma
gets better. I can send her money for the
stage back."

"That won't be necessary." Parker

counted a generous stack of bills onto the
table. "Your wife will be needing a round-
trip ticket and money for expenses while
she's gone?"

"Yes, sir. . . . Mr. Sentell, I—"

Parker handed him the money. "Don't
argue with the boss. You're one of my
best workers, and if you have a need, I
want to know about it."

Chester accepted the money with a
humble, "Thank you, sir. You be sure and
hold it out of my next pay."

Parker closed the desk drawer. "That's
not necessary. We'll settle up when things
are back to normal for you."

"I really appreciate it, Mr. Sentell."
Chester reached to shake his hand. "Can
I put my *X* on a paper for you?"

"No, you take care of your family's
needs."

"Much obliged." Chester put his frayed
hat back on and turned to leave.

"Chester." Parker stopped him. "There
is one thing you can do for me."

"Yes, sir?"

"See if you can find Simon. Tell him I
need to speak to him."

"I shore will, Mr. Sentell." Chester left, closing the door behind him.

Parker turned back to the window. He wished mere money could ease the orphans' problems as easily as it had Chester's.

⁓

Six weeks. June had been in Seattle six weeks, and Sunday camp services were growing. She felt a tingle of anticipation as she unloaded the picnic hamper and located a nice big tree near the riverbank. Twenty had attended the service this morning, and next week there promised to be even more.

Bright sunshine streamed through bare branches of the old oak. Overhead a red-tailed hawk soared to catch the light breeze.

June unpacked the wicker picnic hamper, keeping an eye on Simon and Sam. The besotted couple strolled the banks of the running stream, hand in hand.

Setting a loaf of bread on the blanket, June wondered how love happened so quickly. Sam had known Simon such a short time, but already the two were inseparable.

According to Sam, Simon could quite probably be the man she wanted to spend the rest of her life with, although June didn't see how anyone could arrive at such a significant decision in so brief a time. She smiled, remembering Eli. Of course, she had come hundreds of miles to marry a man she'd never met.

Unscrewing the lid from a jar from Ettie's pantry, she extracted a pickle, then leaned back, biting into its sweetness. Juice squirted and ran down her chin. She lapped it off with her tongue, wondering if she'd ever find love as easily as Sam had.

Simon's eyes had lit up like Christmas candles when Sam invited him to share their lunch after today's services. He readily agreed, and from that moment on, June ceased to exist in the couple's eyes. She was now reduced to watching the picnic basket.

She took another bite of her pickle, sitting up straighter when she saw Parker covering the distance on horseback.

Now there was a man not easily swayed by love. She blushed when she recalled how effortlessly he'd refused Sam's invitation to join them today. Apparently business held a higher priority than his stomach.

Swinging off the stallion, he nodded toward her.

Hoisting the glass pint jar, she smiled. "Pickle?"

To her surprise, he took one and bit it in two. "Good. You make them?"

"No, Ettie did." She was tempted to add that hers were just as good, but she didn't. That would be bragging.

Parker finished the pickle, his eyes focused on Simon, who was skipping stones across the water. "Do those two know it's lunchtime?"

June laughed. "Food is the last thing on their mind."

"Simon not thinking about his next meal? It must be love."

Fishing in the basket, June took out a plate of thickly sliced ham. She set out potato salad, pickled beets, deviled eggs, and a bowl of beans and bacon swimming in blackstrap molasses.

"Change your mind about joining us?" June asked lightly. She didn't want to make much over the fact he'd decided to come, for somewhere deep within her, she relished the unexpected treat. When Parker tried, which admittedly wasn't that often, he could be quite pleasant.

"Not exactly. Business brings me out this way, but there's no reason I can't stay and eat."

June handed him a filled plate. He studied the mound of ham and potato salad, frowning. "You could spoil a man, Miss Kallahan."

She smiled, thinking if that's all it took, he would be an easy man to spoil. She filled a plate for herself as Parker sat down. They bowed their heads, and he said grace.

Unfolding his napkin, Parker said, "Shouldn't the lovebirds be warned we're starting without them?"

June took a bite of ham, chewing thoughtfully. "Do you think they care?"

He chuckled. "Not really."

They managed to carry on a pleasant conversation about the weather and topics that required little thought for the remainder of the meal. Polishing off the last of his potato salad, Parker lifted the lid on the wicker basket and looked inside. "You don't happen to have a chocolate cake in here, do you?"

"No, apple pie." Though Sam had wanted to fix lunch, the orphanage couldn't spare the food. So Ettie had allowed June to commandeer the kitchen this morning. The pie was baked and cooling by the time the sun came up.

Two sizable slices later, Parker lay back against the tree trunk and closed his eyes. June was happy to see he'd loosened his belt a couple of notches. "That, Miss Kallahan, was one fine meal."

"Thank you, Mr. Sentell, but I happen to know Mary is an excellent cook. I ate one of her cinnamon rolls before services this morning, and I've tasted none better."

"Yes," he murmured drowsily. "Mary's a good cook, but I can't remember when I've eaten a better apple pie. Reminds me of my mother's cooking."

She couldn't think of any higher praise. "Cinnamon."

He cracked one eye open to look at her.

"I use extra cinnamon—and chunks of fresh-churned butter."

"Well, keep it up." His eyes drifted closed again.

"Does your mother live around here?"

"No. She's been dead for many years."

June settled back, listening to the birds chirping overhead. "This is my favorite time of year. What about you?"

"It's all right." He appeared to doze, but she knew he wasn't sleeping. She studied the large hands folded contentedly over his broad chest. He always looked clean and freshly shaven. She wondered how he did that. Did someone do his laundry for him? If so, who?

"Mary," he said.

"Huh? . . . What did you say?"

"Mary does my shirts. I pay her to clean once a month and do my laundry."

She blushed. Now *how* did he know what she was thinking?

"You have an expressive face," he answered, tiny lines appearing at his eyes. If she didn't know better, she'd swear he was about to laugh.

Straightening, she covered the bowl of potato salad. In the future she would have to guard her thoughts more carefully.

Silence closed around them. Birds fluttered in and out of tree branches. Sam and Simon had wandered farther down the creek, but they were still in sight.

Shaping her hands into a pillow, June rested her head on the blanket. Here she was, in the company of a very handsome man, and she had put him to sleep.

Full of potato salad, she, too, started to succumb to drowsiness.

"You're doing a good job."

Starting, she lifted her head. Bright sunshine blinded her. "Did you say something?"

"I said, you're doing a good job. The women—and men, too—appreciate Sunday services. I was wrong."

She sat up, basking in his compliment. "Well, thank you. I enjoy leading the services. I haven't started services in other camps yet—but I will." She glanced over and saw his eyes were still closed. "I'm sorry we disagreed about it."

"Don't be sorry. I like a woman who knows her mind and isn't afraid to speak it."

It was just too much. Both compliments *and* praise from Parker Sentell?

"Is that ham I smell?"

June looked up to see Simon and Sam approaching, contented smiles on their faces.

"Parker?" Simon grinned. "Thought you were working."

Without opening his eyes, Parker grunted. "All work and no play makes a man—"

"Dull," Sam finished. She winked at June. "Ain't that right, lovey?"

~

"You don't have to see me home."

Simon ignored Sam's protests as he hitched the buggy. "It'll be raining soon. I'll see that Sissy is brought back to the orphanage." He winked at Parker. "Parker and I have nothing better to do than see you ladies home."

June glanced at Parker, who was tying the mares to the back of the wagon. "Are you sure?" What about that business he'd mentioned?

Straightening, Parker came around the buggy. "Rain's coming up. Don't want you to get wet." He helped her aboard, then took the seat beside her. She felt very small and very important sitting beside him—almost as if they were courting. The thought made her laugh out loud.

Parker turned to look at her. "Care to share what's funny?"

She shook her head. No, she did not care to share that. Not with him.

The orphanage came into view half an hour later.

"Oh, Sam!" June exclaimed. "I'll finally get to meet your aunt."

When the buggy rolled to a stop in front of the towering old house, children poured out the door. June caught herself before she jumped to the ground to run to them. The children ranged from early teens to a blond-haired, blue-eyed toddler.

A frail woman with a mass of snow white hair appeared in the doorway, holding on to the doorframe. She squinted. "Is that you, Sam?"

" 'Tis me, Auntie." Sam waited until Simon lifted her down. "Come meet me dear ol' auntie and the children." She extended a hand to June.

An elderly man carrying an ax came around the corner.

"Hi, Joe—just me, and me friends. Come meet them!"

The old man approached, his faded eyes taking in the newcomers.

"Chopping wood again?" Sam asked.

Joe nodded. "Running low."

June took in the squalor, appalled. The roof was patched in so many places it looked warped. Random placement of large sheets of tin were held down by rocks, adding to the dilapidated appearance.

A young boy edged out to meet them. His solemn brown eyes stared up at June. He was painfully thin, and barefoot.

"Hello." She smiled. "What's your name?"

"Peter."

"Peter. That's a wonderful name."

"It's from the Bible."

June nodded. "I recognized that. Peter, one of Jesus' disciples."

Some of the smaller children held back. They cowered behind Angeline, peeking around her skirt.

Sam urged her friends closer to the house. "Aunt Angeline, I want you to meet June, my friend, and Simon"—Sam's face flamed—"the man I've been telling you about." She blushed, her freckles standing out like measles.

Simon shook hands with Angeline. "Good to see you again, Angeline."

Angeline smiled at the big lumberjack. "Where you been keepin' yourself lately? Haven't seen you around."

Sam's eyes widened. "Do you know me old auntie?"

Simon nodded. "We've met."

June stepped forward to shake the old woman's hand. "Sam's told me so much about you. It's nice to finally meet you."

The old woman's tired eyes looked the young people over. "Good to see you, Parker. Can't thank you enough for all those supplies you been dropping by. Couldn't make it without them."

Parker nodded. "The men want to do more, Angeline."

June turned to look at him. "You know Sam's aunt too?"

He smiled at Angeline. "I manage to get out here every now and then."

June glanced at him accusingly.

"Good of you to bring my niece home, Parker. Won't you come in and sit a spell?"

Simon gave Sam a warm smile. "I'd like that, but it looks as if a storm's about to break. We best be going along."

While Simon and Sam took a private moment to say good-bye, Parker took June's arm and led her back to the buggy. June smiled over her shoulder at the orphans. She'd never seen a more pitiful lot.

"The children break my heart," she whispered. "Sam said the orphans' situation was deplorable, but I've never seen children living in such poor surroundings."

"The community does all it can, under the circumstances." June was glad that he didn't directly accuse Reverend Inman of taking food out of the children's mouths, although the implication was thinly veiled. "Someone needs to step in, close the orphanage down, and find the kids foster homes."

When they drove away a few minutes later, June was still looking over her shoulder, appalled by the sight. One thing was certain—she would be keeping her promise to help Sam all she could. And she would be starting first thing tomorrow morning.

Chapter Nine

Simon's massive frame darkened the office doorway Monday morning. "You wanted to see me, boss?"

Parker motioned for his clerk to sit down.

The chair squeaked under Simon's considerable bulk. "Got a problem?"

A problem? Yes, there was a problem. His name was Isaac Inman. "Something's been bothering me."

Simon's brows knotted with concern. "You comin' down with something?"

Parker shook his head. "I wish the solution were that simple."

Simon leaned back, scissoring his arms

behind his head. "You're thinking about those kids, aren't you?"

Parker turned to the window to look out. Simon could read him like an open book. "What are we going to do about that situation?"

"I don't know. I've been praying about it for some time now. It's a pitiful situation out there."

"It's despicable the way the kids are forced to do without basic necessities. Things we take for granted—food, shelter, clothing—warm clothing that hasn't been worn threadbare by others first. A decent-fitting pair of shoes—shoes that don't rub their feet raw by the end of the day."

"They deserve better," Simon agreed. "They need proper schooling, a chance to learn to read, write, and do arithmetic. Maybe study history."

A muscle tightened in Parker's jaw. "Children need a penny's worth of candy every once in a while. Jawbreakers, lico- rice whips, jelly beans, or peppermint sticks. I've watched the orphans at the mercantile. They stand back, pretending not to care, when you know they do."

Simon shook his head. "There sure

should be something we can do. The men are concerned about the situation, but Inman's got them all fired up about building that tabernacle. Then June caught their eye. They're partial to 'God's little emissary.' Their spare coins go to her."

Parker stared out the window, wracking his brain. The loggers were a generous lot, but Simon was right. Their minds were on the tabernacle.

"I know Angeline would appreciate any help she could get." Simon paused for a long moment. "I noticed a lot of things yesterday that needed fixing, but when it comes down to it, money is what they need most."

"Yes, money would solve a lot of problems."

Simon absently scanned a work order. "Those children haven't had the proper food for years."

Dropping into his chair, Parker propped his boots on the desk. "Or anything else they need."

"True. Well, I'm willing to pitch in a month's pay. If we explain the kids' needs to the men, they'll chip in all they can."

"I have a better idea."

Simon met Parker's steady gaze. "What's that?"

"Inman could help out here."

"Reverend Inman?" Simon frowned. "You can't be serious."

Parker felt his blood pressure rise. "Yes, I'm serious. Why not? He needs to think of the community's needs first, for a change."

"There you go again, boss—you're bull-headed, you know that? You judge every evangelist by your Uncle Walt's shortcomings. You know the reverend feels he's been called by God to build that tabernacle. That doesn't make him crooked."

"We're not talking about my Uncle Walt," Parker snapped. "We're talking about the orphanage. Isaac should see the need without having to point it out to him. After all, it's his community."

"And we're all God's children." Simon shook his head. "Isaac's a good man, whether you want to believe it or not. I've talked to his people. They say he's the salt of the earth, will do anything in his power to serve the Lord. But he's fixed on erecting that tabernacle in his wife's memory. No doubt he sees the orphanage's need, undoubtedly sympathizes with them, but he won't stand for a penny of the contributions to go toward the orphanage—you know that."

"And that's Christianity?"

"Well, Christianity walks a fine line. In one man's mind, what Isaac's doing is the height of servitude; in another's, it's heresy. Men like Isaac confront needs every day—dire, unimaginable needs. Inman's not a miracle worker, Parker; he's one man, a man with a mission—a worthy mission, whether you like it or not. The tabernacle will serve thousands, the orphanage only a handful of children."

"Only a handful of children." Parker found that a bit ironic. "Wonder if that's how God sees it—only a handful of his children?"

Simon got up to pour a cup of coffee. "We could argue all day about what's needed where, and the most, and never come up with a solution. It's up to you and me to find a way to help these particular children." He warmed Parker's cup, then set the pot back on the stove.

Parker sat for a long moment without speaking. The church served the community. The community's future lay with its children. Isaac was obsessed with building the tabernacle, blinded by intent. Couldn't anyone else see that?

"I'm going to have a talk with Isaac."

"You? Talk to Isaac? That would be a first. Thought you didn't approve of him or the tabernacle."

"I don't, but he serves the community's spiritual needs, and the orphans are part of the community. For too long he's turned his back on them. Someone needs to point that out to him."

Simon stirred sugar into his coffee. "The tabernacle's blinded Isaac to a lot of needs."

Parker pushed away from the desk, stretching. "I'll talk to him. If he doesn't like it, that's his problem. Meantime, we're going to have to do more. Have the men take up an offering and send it over to the orphanage—or have Miss Kallahan deliver it."

Simon grinned, and Parker gave him a sour look. "Something funny?"

"Yeah, you and Miss Kallahan. You cross swords more than Sioux warriors. What's wrong with you? She's a pretty woman—available now that Eli's gone. You're single. Why do you want to argue with her?"

"Let's just say I don't like pushy women."

Simon grinned, then quickly recovered when Parker shot him a dark look. He watched his boss drain his cup and set it on the desk, then shrug into his coat.

"Think I'll have that talk with Isaac while it's on my mind. Can you take care of things here while I'm gone?"

"I'll give it a try. If you see Sam, tell her I said hello."

Parker paused at the door. "Seems to me you're getting mighty interested in Sam Harris all of a sudden."

Simon took a sip of coffee, grinning. "Seems that way to me, too."

"Sam's worried about your shyness—thinks the cat gets your tongue."

Simon scowled. "Who told you that?"

"I overheard June and Mary discussing it the other day."

"Women!" Simon shuffled the work orders. "You know talking to women don't come easy for me—except talking to Sam.

I feel comfortable around her, even if I don't talk her leg off."

Parker frowned. "If it's talking you're worried about, you should have Miss Kallahan help you with that. She talks enough for two people."

"Isaac, I want to talk to you."

Isaac glanced up, and upon seeing Parker standing in the doorway, returned to the papers he was reading. "That's surprising, since you haven't been so inclined now for several years."

Parker ignored the rebuke. He wasn't here for scones and a tea party. "I want to discuss the orphanage."

Isaac frowned. "The orphanage. Is that all that's on people's minds these days? The orphanage has been here for years. Why all the sudden concern? The children are healthy, aren't they? They have a roof over their head, and food on the table."

"Healthy, maybe; food, occasionally. The roof's a laugh. Something has to be done about their situation."

"I have no argument with that, but you must realize there are so many—"

Parker's deadly tone stopped him. "Cut it out, Isaac. It's me—Parker. Remember? Of course there are many needs, but the orphans are *our* particular problem. I want your ministry to help them."

Removing his glasses, Isaac polished them, refusing to look up. "How can I help?"

"Give the orphans at least one Sunday-night offering a month. That's an insignificant amount compared to the overall picture. The kids will have proper food and clothing, and the community can rest in the knowledge they are taking care of their own."

Isaac stuffed the handkerchief in his pocket, his features tight. "I'll have the elders prepare more food baskets and deliver them—"

"The children need more than food baskets. They need a steady income. The old woman is sick. She isn't able to drum up donations like she used to. Provide those kids funding, Isaac. If the tabernacle is God's plan, he will see it built."

Isaac's eyes centered on the window, where outside a gray drizzle fell. "My heart goes out to those children—to needy children throughout the world. If I could, I would see to it that not one single child would go to bed hungry tonight. But it isn't within my power. I'm only one man, Parker. You must know a minister's task is overwhelming. As much as I want to help, I cannot take money from the crusade and give it for another cause, no matter how worthy that cause might be. Donations received from this ministry must go to build the tabernacle."

A suffocating tightness squeezed Parker's chest. *Remember, you're here for the orphans, not to chastise Isaac,* he reminded himself.

"You're wrong, Isaac. You know that. My men do all they can, but they're following you, and forgetting their responsibilities toward those less fortunate."

Parker saw the way the loggers gave outside the saloon, but all collected funds were channeled toward the tabernacle. The orphans were getting trampled in the shuffle.

Isaac stared straight ahead, refusing to meet Parker's eyes. "I wish I could help, but I stand firm in my conviction—my knowledge of what I have been called to do."

They were getting nowhere. "Those children need your help. Read your Bible."

"I am aware of their needs, and I read my Bible daily, thank you. I am concerned about the orphans, but God has called me for a different purpose. God has called me to build a tabernacle. I will abide in his Word and see my mission accomplished. I must keep my eyes focused on the tabernacle. A place of worship that will feed the spiritual needs of thousands, not just the everyday needs of a few."

"OK." Parker realized he couldn't argue with a fence post. Isaac's mind was made up. If the children were to eat properly, he'd have to find another avenue. "I hope *you* can sleep warm tonight, Isaac, and aren't kept awake by the knowledge there are babies down the road who can't."

Isaac never raised his eyes. Parker walked out.

Chapter Ten

Mary, what a pretty necklace!" June admired the chain of colorful glass beads before handing it to Sam. "Did you make this?"

Mary blushed. "Oh, it's nothing, really."

"Ow, lovey, it's smashin', it is! I didn't know you did such handiwork!"

Color deepened in Mary's cheeks. "Oh, go on—it's only cheap baubles woven onto golden thread. My grandmother taught me how to do it."

Sam closely examined the trinket, her eyes bright with admiration. "Where do you get such lovely beads?"

"Oh, my Eddie buys them when he

goes to visit his mother in Spokane. I'll make you one, if you like.''

''I'd love it!'' Sam grabbed the skinny cook around the neck and hugged her. ''It would be ever so nice o' you.''

Mary glanced at June. ''I'll make you one too. I'll have them both finished by next Sunday.''

The women admired the necklace as the cookshack filled with morning worshipers. Twenty-eight, in all, sat around the long table. June mentally calculated the multicolored paper chains left in her box, glad she'd brought extra.

After services, June and Sam repacked the box, and Simon carried it back to the wagon. June looked the other way when Sam leaned over and whispered something in Simon's ear. The gentle giant turned beet red and nodded.

''What did you say to him?'' June whispered under her breath as they walked off.

''I told 'im 'e looked right smashing today, 'e did, and told 'im 'e looked good enough to kiss.''

''Oh, Sam.'' June punched her in the side. ''Stop—you'll embarrass the poor man.''

"Too late." Sam's features turned solemn. "Already did." The women burst into laughter, June's fading when she spotted Parker through the office window. He was leaning back, boots on the desk, engrossed in a handful of papers.

"Ow, look, lovey." Sam punched her. "There's your sweetie."

Sweetie, June scoffed, ignoring Sam's mischievous grin. Parker wasn't her sweetie—though the thought wasn't that unappealing.

"Oh, Sam, I wish he would just once look at me the way Simon looks at you."

"Maybe 'e would, if you'd be a bit more friendly."

"I try to be friendly, Sam. He just plain doesn't like me. Since I'm working with the crusade, he equates me with Reverend Inman. It's so unfair. Parker acts as if Reverend Inman doesn't care about anything but the tabernacle, but it's not true. Reverend Inman mentioned the orphanage twice this week, and just yesterday he sent Ben over with two bushels of apples and three hams."

Sam tsked. "Such a pity. Hardheaded as a rock."

"Those two remind me of hardheaded Christians who—" June's footsteps slowed, and she turned to face Sam. "Why, that's exactly what they remind me of. I hadn't realized it until this very moment, but Reverend Inman and Parker have forgotten what Christians are supposed to do when one or the other is overcome by sin. They are to gently and humbly help that person back onto the right path. Reverend Inman and Parker are trampling each other in their efforts to prove the other wrong!"

"Don't know what you can do 'bout it. Until they both realize what they're doing, their warrin' won't cease."

June gathered her skirt and climbed into the wagon. "That may be, but perhaps it's my duty to remind them." Sam took her place on the board seat beside her. June continued, "It was nice of Mary to offer to make us a necklace. They are lovely."

"Breathtakin', to be sure," Sam agreed. "I wouldn't have thought poor little Mary was so talented, 'er being so mousey and all. Why, what woman wouldn't love to own such a pretty? I've seen nothing in the mercantile like it."

June squealed, hauling back on the reins. Sam grasped June's arm and held on for dear life. "What's wrong? More pigs?"

"No, you! Do you know what you just said?"

Sam frowned. "More pigs?"

"No, before that!"

Sam concentrated, her face a mask of confusion.

June prompted her. "You were talking about Mary's necklace."

"What about it? I said it was pretty—"

"And other women would like it too. You said there's nothing like it in the mercantile!"

Sam released June's arm. "June Kallahan, 'ave you lost your bloomin' mind? What does Mary's necklace 'ave to do with anythin'?"

"Don't you see? I've been wracking my brain for days for a way to raise money for the orphanage other than using crusade funds. We can sell necklaces! Mary said the beads were inexpensive. I have a small nest egg, not much, but if the beads are inexpensive and the necklaces simple to make, perhaps Mary will teach us how."

June sat back, plotting her strategy. "I'll use my savings to buy the beads and thread, and we can sell the necklaces to the loggers. Most all have wives and girl-friends waiting at home. I'll bet the men would love the chance to give their sweet-hearts a present to make up for their ab-sence. And for those who don't have sweethearts, they surely have mothers! Just think, Sam! If business is good, we can buy that stove for the upstairs bed-room in no time at all!"

"But using your life savin's, lovey—are you sure you want to do that?"

"I'm positive! It's not much, but it will multiply threefold if the men like the neck-laces."

"Mary might not be anxious to share 'er secret."

"Oh, but she will, once we explain what we're doing. Come on, Sam! It's a brilliant idea. We'll take the necklace money and use it for the orphans' needs. I won't be taking money from the crusade, so Rever-end Inman can't object, and I won't be angering Parker, because I'm not soliciting donations for Reverend Inman." June flung her arms around Sam and hugged her right there in the middle of the road. "It's perfect!"

"Ow, I don't know, lovey." Sam pried June's arms loose, choking.

"We'll talk to Mary." June reached for the reins and wheeled the buggy around in the middle of the road.

"Now? But I'm hungry!" The clattering wagon drowned out Sam's protests.

June gripped the reins and planted her feet. This was too important to wait. Much too important!

Within a month, necklace sales had exceeded June's wildest expectations. Mary had opened her heart and her cookshack to assemble the colorful trinkets, and the men opened their wallets and splurged on the jewelry. Luther Medsker even bought one for his mother-in-law.

Lying back on her bed, June thought of all the exhausting work she, Sam, and Mary had put into the entrepreneurial venture. But it was paying off! In just the past three days they had collected over thirty dollars. This morning June was taking the oldest children to the mercantile to be fitted for new shoes. And not one cent had come out of the tabernacle fund.

Glory be to God! June hugged her pillow, elated with the progress. In no time at all, the children would have the new stove *and* winter coats.

The mercantile was empty when June led three children in later that morning. Peter shot straight to the shoe rack and began inspecting the merchandise, his eyes wide with wonder. Allowing the others equal time to browse, June purchased peppermint sticks for the smaller children.

"I threw in a couple of extra sticks," the clerk confessed with a conspirator's wink.

"Thank you." June smiled. "You can't possibly know how much your kindness will be appreciated."

Picking up a bolt of red hair ribbon, she laid it on the counter. The girls would have a squealing fit when she tied the ribbon in their hair tonight.

Stepping to the Home Fire stove displayed on a wooden platform, she admired it. It was a fine stove—the finest she'd ever seen. Running her hands over

the shiny cast iron, she mentally calculated how many necklaces she would
have to sell in order to purchase it. A lot,
she decided, after numerous attempts to
cipher the amount.

The front door opened, and June
glanced up to see Reverend Inman coming in. The reverend took off his hat, his
eyes casting about the room. When he
spotted June, he broke into a smile.
"June!"

"Good morning, Reverend," June
called.

Reverend Inman hurried over to her,
mopping his brow. "It's too soon to be
this warm." His eyes brightened when he
saw the orphans. "My, my. Who have we
here?"

The children gathered around the minister, the youngest hanging on to his leg.

"What brings you children out on such
a warm day?"

"We're gettin' new shoes!" they cho-
rused.

"New shoes!" Reverend Inman looked
surprised. He addressed the storekeeper.
"I think we should have three of those

nice, plump candy balls to go with those new shoes, don't you, children?"

The children nodded their unanimous, enthusiastic endorsement.

Reverend Inman dug in his pocket and laid a coin on the counter. "Let the children select the color they want."

The clerk nodded. "Come along, children. Who wants a red one?"

"Me, me," they clamored. Footsteps echoed across the wood floor as they made a beeline for the candy jar.

June turned back to face Reverend Inman. "That's generous of you, Reverend. The children rarely get such a treat."

Reverend Inman's eyes followed the children and softened with compassion. "Poor tykes. I wish I could do more."

June selected a tin of sugar and laid it on the counter. "What brings you to town so early?"

"Ettie's running low on coffee. I promised to bring some home before dinnertime." Reverend Inman glanced at the bolt of red ribbon and the peppermint sticks lying on the counter. "Looks like you're doing quite a lot of shopping today." He turned to look at the children, who were busy now trying on the new purchases. "Did the orphanage come into a windfall?"

"Oh, no," June said. She paused, biting her lower lip. She'd supposed he'd already heard about the necklaces she had been selling. But perhaps he was so preoccupied with crusade business that he hadn't heard. "No windfall."

His features sobered. "You're not using tabernacle funds, are you? I thought we'd discussed this and agreed where our priorities lie."

"We did—and I'm not using ministry funds without your knowledge. I wouldn't do that."

Reverend Inman's eyes swept the room, the children, the peppermint sticks, and the red ribbons. "Then where is all this money coming from?" June was troubled to hear a note of urgency in his voice.

"Sam, Mary, and I have been selling necklaces."

Reverend Inman's brow lifted. "Selling necklaces?"

"Just frivolous trinkets. The men buy them for their sweethearts. The money

from the necklaces goes toward the orphanage."

She wanted to make it abundantly clear
that the orphanage proceeds had absolutely nothing to do with tabernacle funds.

A shadow crossed Reverend Inman's
face. "No wonder I don't see you around
very often. You must keep very busy, collecting funds for both the orphanage and
the tabernacle. That's quite an undertak-
ing for one person."

June couldn't miss the new coolness in
his voice. "Not really—I have plenty of
time for both."

He gazed down his nose at her, his features stern. "Perhaps, but I wouldn't think
you could do proper service to two
causes. Do you?"

"Yes, sir, I think I can. I work as hard
for one as I do for the other." Opening the
string on her purse, she rummaged
around and came up with a handful of
coins. "I collected this in front of The
Gilded Hen yesterday. You can see the
men's dedication to the building fund
hasn't changed."

Reverend Inman lowered his voice. His
features took a somber look. "June, it

isn't the money. It's your loyalty I seek.
You are being torn between two needs—
both great, both important. While I ap-
plaud your generosity, I wonder about
your motives. Giving has dropped off
lately. This concerns me greatly. What
would Eli think of you funneling money
away from the crusade?''

June dropped her eyes submissively. "I
would never do that.''

"This must stop. Immediately.''

The force of his words stunned her. He
couldn't mean that he believed she would
take from the tabernacle funds. ''Are you
asking me to choose between the orphans
and the ministry?''

*Please, God, don't let him be asking
that.* The choice would be impossible.
Both were just causes. Why couldn't Reverend Inman—or Parker, for that matter—
see that?

The front door opened, and as if the
devil had summoned help to further her
dilemma, Parker and two other men
walked in. When Parker spotted her and
the reverend, he stalked to the back of the
store.

"I'd best be getting that coffee to Ettie.'' Reverend Inman selected a tin and set it on the counter.

"I'm sorry, Reverend."

Reverend Inman turned away, directing his attention to the clerk.

Edging to the back of the store, June sought out Parker. As gruff as he could be, she needed his insight. She needed to know why he was so against Reverend Inman. Did he see something that she was blind to?

Parker was squatting on his haunches, sorting through a pile of hand implements, when June came up to him.

"Miss Kallahan."

"I didn't expect to see you here this morning."

He glanced up. "That makes two of us." He returned to the job at hand.

"Can I ask you something?"

"Since when do you need permission to ask me anything?"

Casting a glance toward the front of the store, she lowered her voice. "It's about Reverend Inman."

Parker didn't look up. "What about him?"

Kneeling beside him, she dropped her voice to a whisper. "I'm puzzled. I know you don't approve of Reverend Inman or the tabernacle. You don't attend services as often as you should. On top of that, Eli was your best friend, and Eli shared Reverend Inman's dream—to the extent that he worked through all sorts of weather, acquiring donations to build the temple— literally giving his *life* in order to achieve the dream. How can you explain all this?"

Parker sorted through the hand tools. "Why do I have to explain it?"

"Well, because. I think you and I are at odds over something, but I'm not sure what. Don't you think it would profit both of us if *I* knew what we were arguing about?"

Shoving a hammer aside, Parker looked at her. Anger darkened his eyes, and she wondered if she was wise to confront him—yet she had to know. Why was he so dead set against Reverend Inman's efforts?

"Men like Isaac burn me."

She stared back at him. "Burn you? What do you mean?"

"I had an uncle like Isaac. Man of the pulpit, smooth talker, fleecing the flock for money to be used for *his* glory."

June's heart sank. Nobody wanted to confront the issue of an evangelist who'd lost his way. It happened, but no Christian was proud of it. Bad things happened.

"And you think that's what Reverend Inman's doing?"

His gaze met hers stoically. "What do *you* think? God doesn't require that great monuments be built in his name."

"No, that's true. But is it wrong for Christians to honor their Lord by erecting churches befitting his name?"

Parker shook his head. "I'm not going to argue religion, Miss Kallahan. I read my Bible. I know what's commanded of us."

"So, you're saying that as Christians, we should interpret God's Word only as he reveals it to us."

"That's what I'm saying."

"Good, because this is a good place to remind you to read Galatians 6. Then come back, and we'll discuss this rationally. Did you feel this way about Eli's involvement with the tabernacle?"

"Eli knew how I felt about the tabernacle."

"You talked about it?"

"Many times, but I knew Eli's heart was in the right place. Eli let Isaac influence him. Isaac let his wife, Katherine, influence him. It was a bad mix."

"Have you spoken to Reverend Inman about your feelings?"

He gave her a sour look.

"You haven't, have you?"

"I haven't spoken to Isaac about anything other than the orphans. I must say, Miss Kallahan, his true spirit was evident."

June ignored his sarcasm. "Well, shame on both of you. You're Christian men acting like children. You should be working just as hard to build the tabernacle and support the orphanage as I am."

Impatience flared in his eyes. "I wouldn't collect a penny for Isaac."

"Ah—then you're judging."

"No, I'm not judging. That's my opinion."

"And your opinion is, all evangelists—Reverend Inman included—are dishonest."

"I didn't say that."

"But you did. You said your uncle was confused, lost his way; therefore, all evangelists are bad."

Parker stood up. "I *didn't* say that!" A logger examining a flannel shirt turned to stare at them.

June rose to face Parker. "You did too!" She controlled the impulse to raise her voice. She could see she was severely testing his control. Good. She wanted him to stop and think about his prejudices and put a face on them.

"I am saying, Miss Kallahan, that I think there are far more pressing needs in this world than erecting an expensive monument meant to glorify Isaac Inman's name."

"And that's the only reason you forbid me to take up a collection in your camp on Sunday?"

He crossed his arms. "That's precisely why."

"But you agree there are other needs, more worthy needs even in your eyes, when a collection is acceptable."

"Of course. I know it takes money to carry on God's work."

"Then you wouldn't care if I took up a collection for—say—the orphans, on Sunday mornings."

"Why would I object to that?"

"I don't know. Would you?"

"No."

"Then I can?"

His eyes narrowed with suspicion. "Why do I have the impression I've just been had?"

She grinned. "A tiny collection—to go toward the orphans' needs alone." She couldn't sell necklaces anymore, not without risking Reverend Inman's disapproval. She had to regain those funds some way.

She thought she detected a tolerant smile twitching at the corners of Parker's mouth. But she couldn't be sure. It would be so unlike him to smile.

"All right. You can take a collection for the orphans on Sunday mornings, but don't think for one minute you've talked me into anything. I was just getting ready to suggest the idea myself."

She presented her most somber face. "No, I would never think that."

Nodding, he picked up a shovel and

walked to the counter. Reverend Inman and Parker eyed each other disagreeably.

"Good morning, Sentell."

"Morning, Reverend."

Reverend Inman paid for his purchase, tipped his hat to Parker, and left the store. The door closed behind Parker a moment later.

Those two need to talk, June decided, unwrapping a peppermint stick and taking a lick. They were both wrong.

Chapter Eleven

I'm worried, June," Sam said as she and June prepared food in the orphanage's kitchen. "I feel like we're running out of space here. You know the wee tykes need not only space but clothes, toys, shoes, books, food. Come winter, they'll need warm coats and mufflers. Where's it all to come from?"

June sighed. "I know. I'm worried too. The extra clothing I collected helped some, but it's not enough. People don't seem to have much left over to give."

"You two worry too much."

Sam and June jumped in surprise. They hadn't heard Simon approach.

"Just feeling a bit sorry for meself, love." Sam stood on tiptoe to accept his kiss. "What brings you out this way today?"

"You." Simon smoothed her creased brow with his forefinger. "I thought we might eat our dinner together."

She grinned, stealing another quick kiss. "Can't think of anything I'd like better."

Simon unknotted the corners of a cloth bag and took out two thick ham sandwiches and laid them on the table. June busied herself making a pot of fresh coffee.

"How're things going?" Simon asked.

"Not so good. The wee ones need so much. The camp offering Parker allows June to take helps, but it's not nearly enough. The roof needs fixing, the baby needs special medicine. . . . The list is endless."

"If Isaac would share a few of his offerings, it would make things easier," Simon grumbled.

June looked at him. So Parker wasn't the only one who felt this way. She herself had begun to feel confused. Hadn't God sent her to Eli, and then to carry on his work? Yet as she saw the needs of the orphans, she felt more and more pulled toward helping them. What was her call? She'd thought she knew, but when Reverend Inman asked her to choose, she began to question everything.

"June's done her best to talk to 'im; Parker's done his best to talk to 'im. But Reverend Inman can't see his responsibility 'ere."

"Then he's blind."

Sam shrugged. " 'e is, in some ways. Can't see beyond 'is wife's dream."

Simon turned to June. "What do you think?"

"I'm not sure," she admitted. "Perhaps the tabernacle Katherine envisioned has become his obsession."

"It's not right. . . . Don't know what the orphans will do when you're forced to shut this place down."

Shut down? Would it come to that? Much as June hated to face it, that did seem the likely scenario—if something more couldn't be done. "There should be a way to support both the orphanage and the tabernacle," she said. "Why does everyone think that's so impossible?"

"Well, it seems like it should be possible, but those kids still need a decent roof over their heads and a stove to warm the upstairs. I know you've been working real hard, Miss June, but still the needs are too great."

Sam turned to Simon, her eyes ablaze. "Well, June's 'elping me not to lose faith in the power of God. Reverend Inman may come through yet."

"I wouldn't hold my breath."

Sam grinned. "That's not sayin' we might not all 'ave to give God a wee bit of 'elp."

Simon lifted his cup, and June filled it with hot coffee. Cocking an ear, Simon listened. "What's all that pounding?"

"Ow, that. Joe's putting a new floor on the back porch. Harold Stinson donated lumber from the old cabin 'e tore down last week."

Sam lifted the curtain window to look out. The children were playing in the yard with the few wooden toys Simon and Joe had made for them. She let the curtain fall back into place. When a knock sounded at the back door, Sam sprang up to answer it.

"Parker! I didn't expect you this morning."

"I hear Joe's working on the porch—" Parker looked over her shoulder. "Simon?"

Simon waved from his place at the table. "Guess you're here to help build the porch too?"

Parker nodded. "Thought Pine Ridge could do without me for a day."

Sam noticed the twinkle in his eyes. "Have you brought someone with you?"

"Oh, there are a couple of wagons outside. They just happen to be full of shingles that my men cut—"

"Shingles!" Sam flung her arms around his neck and held on. "The roof! You're goin' to patch the roof." Sam couldn't imagine not having to sidestep pots in the middle of the floor.

She stepped back, aware Parker was straining to see around her.

June lowered her eyes, blushing at Parker's gaze.

"Hello, June."

My, it was awfully warm in here all of a sudden! "Parker," she said. "How good of you to come and help with the roof."

He smiled at her. Never taking his gaze from her, he said to Sam, "Think I can tear Joe away from the porch long enough to help unload those shingles?"

Sam fairly danced out the back door. "Joe! Come quick! Parker just brought shingles!" She raced back to the table and flung her arms around Simon's neck. "Glory be! You hear that, love? Shingles!"

Looking at Parker, June said, "You have no idea what this means. I wish I could think of some way to thank you."

"The smiles on your faces are thanks enough." Parker glanced at the fresh pot of coffee. "And maybe a cup of whatever that is that smells so good."

Simon finished off his sandwich and stood up. "Guess those shingles won't unload themselves."

Parker settled his hat back on his head. "Guess not."

"And I'll pray that God will hold back the rain until you're finished," June promised.

Before sunup the following morning, Parker and Simon returned with four other loggers in tow. While Angeline rested in her attic room, the men began tearing off the old roof.

Warning the children to stay out of the way, Sam and June planned to cook all morning in preparation for the noon meal. Parker had delivered two boxes of groceries the day before.

"When I unloaded the boxes, guess what I found," Sam asked June.

June couldn't guess.

"Ten whole dollars in the bottom of the basket!" Sam slid four loaves of white bread dough into the oven to bake.

"Who do you think put it there?"

"I 'spect it be Parker—or me Simon. When I asked Simon 'bout it, he just shrugged and said the tooth fairy most likely did it."

"Did you know today is Parker's birthday?" June asked as she wiped a bowl and set it back on the shelf.

"Is it, now?" Sam dumped pea pods into a bucket. "Then we have to do something special for him." She handed one of the orphans, Mary Ann, the bucket. "Empty it outdoors, lovey."

"Well, I know Parker favors chocolate cake."

"Chocolate cake, eh? I'll need to check the pantry, but I think we have the proper ingredients for a chocolate cake."

"I'll make it," Mary Jane volunteered, "if you'll show me how."

"I'll be glad to." June grinned. "I'll tell you what to do, and you do it. It'll be a great surprise for Parker."

June had decided the older girls needed tutoring in the basics of cooking and sewing. Together they'd repaired sheets, learned to darn socks, and were now starting to knit sweaters for the younger children's Christmas presents. June knew it would take all summer to finish the items since most of the girls were under the age of twelve.

Aunt Angeline, though failing, often came downstairs to sit with them, providing a critical eye, advice, or direction on a proper stitch. June enjoyed Angeline's presence. It reminded her of the hours she'd spent under Aunt Thalia's watchful supervision.

With June standing by, Mary Jane sifted

flour, cocoa, baking soda, baking powder, and salt into a large bowl.

Cracking three eggs into the dry ingredients, the child added sugar, vanilla, and thick buttermilk.

In no time at all, a heavenly aroma rose from the oven. Mary Jane skipped off to tell the other orphans about the special treat she'd helped make for Mr. Sentell.

June poured two cups of coffee and took a seat across the table from Sam.

"You're so good at this, lovey. I don't know 'ow you cope so well."

"I love children—I hope to have a whole houseful someday."

"Ever give any thought to who the proud papa will be?"

"If I did, I wouldn't tell you," June teased.

Sam brushed a handful of unruly red locks back from her face. "I wish I had your confidence. Seems I'm having more than me share of doubts of late."

"Simon?" June guessed.

"No, not me Simon. 'e's the salt of the earth, 'e is. No, I'm thinkin' if anything happens to Auntie, I'll have to go back to England."

"And you don't want to?"

"Ow, it's not that I don't love me country; it's just I've grown to love the children. Feel like me own, they do. Would break me 'eart if they had to go to foster homes."

"Yes, I can see that."

"June, when we first came here, we believed God wanted us here. But when we first came, we thought we'd be doing somethin' entirely different than what we're doin' now. Does that mean God was wrong?"

June's eyes softened. "I've wondered the same thing myself, at times. But I do believe that God is never wrong, Sam. He doesn't make mistakes."

Sam took a sip of coffee. "If that be true, then you think he'll make all this trouble and woe work for his glory?"

"I have to believe that. And if Reverend Inman has temporarily lost his way, God will make him aware of it. In his own time."

"I certainly hope so, lovey—I certainly hope so."

Thirty minutes later June stepped out the back door and into a hubbub. The

children danced around in the yard, playing spirited games. Men crawled over the
orphanage like bees on a honeycomb. It
wasn't quite noon yet, and they'd already
torn off half the old roof.

"Dinner's ready," June called.

"Good thing," Parker yelled back.

She shaded her eyes against the sun,
looking up to where he stood on the tall-
est roof peak.

His silhouette was clear against the sky,
and June's heart skipped a beat. He was
incredibly big and strong. They might not
see eye to eye on Reverend Inman or the
tabernacle, but there was a lot of good in
Parker. As hard as he tried to hide it, it
was there. It would be so very easy to fall
in love with this man—She caught her er-
rant thoughts as Aunt Angeline appeared
and slowly made her way to a chair sitting
beneath a tree in the backyard, where she
could oversee the younger children.

"Are you all right, Auntie?" June called.

The old woman waved, covering her lap
with a light blanket.

"She's so frail," Sam fretted as June returned to the kitchen. "But she wants to
'elp."

"I worry about her."

"You shouldn't, love. She's 'ad a good life, and she's lookin' forward to meetin' the Lord. I try to make 'er rest—lately she's been more willing. I think she's just plain wearin' out."

The men washed up and took their places at the large table set up in the backyard. They dug in, filling their plates with roast beef, chicken swimming in rich broth with dumplings, peas, corn, turnips, mashed potatoes, and loaves of fresh-baked bread.

"You're going to make us all fat," Parker teased, shoving back from his plate a while later. June smiled, pleased that he'd eaten four servings of everything.

The men visited for a while to let their food digest. Parker finally stretched, then said, "I guess the work won't get done with us sitting here."

June sprang up. "Don't go yet!" She gave Mary Jane the prearranged signal. Shortly before, three of the older girls had disappeared to the kitchen to slice wedges of chocolate cake with thick fudge icing.

They now carried trays of dessert out to the makeshift tables in the yard.

"What's this?" Simon exclaimed.

"Happy birthday, Parker!" Sam shouted.

Parker looked genuinely stunned and a little embarrassed. His eyes fastened on June. "How did you know?"

"Simon looked it up in the camp records." She blushed. "I hope you don't mind. I always like to know a person's birthday."

He took in the cake and the festive icing as if he still couldn't believe it. "I haven't had a birthday cake since, well, I don't re-member when." He dipped a large spoon into the icing and closed his eyes to savor the taste. "This is good." He opened his eyes, grinning. "Really good."

After dessert the men settled on the porch to rest before climbing back onto the roof. The weather was mild, and some shed their shirts. Some of the boys joined them, and June was appalled when a spit-ting match began.

Although she didn't want to encourage their antics, she couldn't help but see how the little ones gravitated to the men. After a while the older boys took out the pocketknives they had received as Christmas gifts and attempted to carve toys for the younger children. Parker and Simon knelt on the ground, showing them how to carve whistles.

Before long the air resonated with the shrill sounds.

"I hope this doesn't get to be a habit," Sam complained, wincing as another screech split the air.

June laughed. "Isn't it wonderful to see the children having such a good time?"

Soon the sounds of hammers filled the air. The men nailed new shingles on the half of the roof they'd exposed that morning. June helped Sam settle the younger children for naps, though she seriously doubted that sleep was possible with all the racket.

Angeline, though, seemed to have no problem sleeping through the noise.

It was late afternoon when the men came off the roof and settled in the grass to eat sandwiches made from roast beef and bread left over from lunch.

"It's been a good day of work," one of the loggers commented, looking up at the new shingles.

"It's been a very good day of work," Sam agreed. "I wish I could think of some way to thank you for all you've done."

Parker was sitting on the grass, a sandwich in one hand, a glass of cold well water in the other. Sweat ran in rivulets down his face, and he wiped it away with his forearm. June watched, thinking he'd never looked more handsome. He finished the food, stretched, and pushed himself up. He said a few words to the men, smiled June's way, and started toward the front yard.

Groaning, Simon and the other men got to their feet and headed toward the wagons. Sam ran to catch up with Simon.

June quickly ducked into the house, exiting the front door as Parker rounded the corner.

"Parker?"

When he turned, the setting sun washed his face in golden color, defining his rugged features. June inhaled sharply. How handsome he was! "Happy birthday."

"Thank you for the cake," he said. "I don't know when . . ." He paused. "Well, my birthdays come and go with no fuss. In fact, I'd forgotten the date myself."

"How old are you?" she teased. The records said he was twenty-nine.

"Too old for birthday cake," he said dryly.

"Nobody's ever too old for birthday cake." June wished the butterflies fluttering in her stomach would settle down. "I made something for you."

"More surprises?"

She handed him the package and waited while he opened it. He held the quilted squares up to the light, examining them. Her heart sank. Why didn't he say something? Didn't he know what they were? Or did he know and just not like the idea of her giving him a gift?

"They're . . . hand warmers." She stepped closer, aware of his masculine scent, all warm and musky. "See? There's a round stone for each finger. You warm the stones on the rail around the stove, then when you go outside, you slip them inside your gloves. Or when you come inside, you hold the stones for a few minutes to warm your hands—"

He looked up, and she could swear there was a strange mist in his eyes. "I— no one has ever made me a gift."

June smiled. "No one? Ever?"

"No one. Ever. I've been on my own since I was fourteen, June. And even when Ma and Pa were alive . . . well, there were a lot of kids at home." He looked at the hand warmers. "This is . . . the warmers will come in handy come fall and winter. Thank you."

"Happy birthday."

He hesitated, and for a moment she thought he would kiss her. She realized she'd like that, very much. But then he turned on his heel and strode quickly toward the wagon.

Think of me, Parker, every time you see those hand warmers, every time you hold them.

She returned to the house to finish cleaning up the kitchen, wondering what kind of childhood Parker had endured. If he'd never been given a gift, if birthday surprises were foreign to him, no wonder he was so touched by the orphans' plight.

No wonder he found a tabernacle a poor substitute for caring for God's children.

"Parker Sentell, if you belonged to me, you'd have gifts every day of the week,"

she whispered as she poured boiling water into the sudsy dishpan. "And I'd bake
chocolate cakes and apple pies until they
were coming out your ears. We'd worship
in an open field every Sunday morning, if
that suited you."

She washed a cup and set it aside to
drain dry. "God loves you; Eli loved you,
Parker Sentell. And I could love you too, if
you'd let me."

Chapter Twelve

No matter how bad things are, they can always get worse.

Until yesterday June hadn't thought much about Aunt Thalia's old adage, but today it was back to haunt her.

Standing beneath an umbrella, she listened to Reverend Inman recite Psalm 23 to the small group of assembled mourners. Overnight, things had gotten worse. Much worse.

"The Lord is my shepherd; I shall not want. He maketh me to lie down in green pastures: he leadeth me beside the still waters. He restoreth my soul. . . ."

The fiery man of God's Word seemed

uncharacteristically subdued this morning as Reverend Inman finalized Angeline's simple graveside service with a heartfelt whispered "Amen and amen."

June drew Sam into the comfort of her arms while the young girl sobbed quietly into a frayed hankie. Rain clouds hovered overhead, and the mourners sank deeper into the lining of their coats. A cold rain began to fall.

June focused on the mourners gathered to eulogize Angeline Ferriman, the woman known to many as "that poor soul responsible for all those children."

In life Angeline hadn't cultivated many close friendships; in death, neighbors and community members gathered to pay homage to the slightly eccentric woman who had run the local orphanage. Heads bowed, dressed in Sunday best and spit-shined shoes, they stood before the simple casket and prayed.

Where had they been when Aunt Angie was alive and in desperate need of their help? June wondered.

"Judge not, that ye be not judged." Jesus' words shamed her thoughts, and she banished them, wondering instead

how Sam would keep the children together now that Angeline was gone.

Ol' Joe stood next to June, dressed in a
thin coat that afforded little protection
from the chilly wind. The children huddled
in a group on his right side, bracing themselves against the driving rain.

It seemed to June the person who'd
known Aunt Angie the least was taking her
passing the hardest. Tears rolled down
Ben Wilson's face as he stared at the casket.

Death had come swiftly for Angeline.
Though everyone suspected she had been
failing for some time, her passing came as
a shock. Perhaps it always does, June
thought.

Angeline had asked to be buried at the
edge of her property, beneath a large
Douglas fir she'd planted herself, forty-two
springs ago.

Pallbearers, some who had been with
Reverend Inman's crusade in the earlier
days when he traveled, others from Pine
Ridge Logging Camp, gently lowered the
plain pine coffin into the muddy ground.

June was painfully aware of the children's tear-streaked faces. Though Aunt

Angeline had taught them about the Good Book, the joys of Christianity, death, and heaven, most were too young to comprehend.

The older ones understood enough to know that Aunt Angie was never coming back. June wondered about the anguish, the multitude of questions and fears that must be playing through their minds.

When the last prayer was issued, Simon stepped forward and led a weeping Sam from the gravesite.

June was surprised and grateful when Parker took her arm, and they fell into step behind the young couple.

"Terrible day for a funeral," he observed quietly.

"Sam's taking her aunt's death awfully hard."

"Well, she's here in a strange community, her family overseas. I imagine she's scared."

"She'd grown very close to Angeline."

"There must be something more I can do to help," Parker said.

June paused, turning to look at him. He constantly surprised her with his compassion. "If you truly mean that, I'm sure there is."

"You need only to let me know what's needed." He reached for her hand, and his eyes softened as he clasped it tightly in his. "I'll do what's possible to keep the children together. Simon and I have already discussed it."

June's stomach felt all knotted and strange, a feeling she often had in Parker's presence these days.

She squeezed his hand, thankful for his comforting presence.

The townspeople provided food for the bereaved. The orphanage's huge oak table held more food than the children had ever seen at one time, yet the children didn't seem eager to eat. They sat or stood staring, seemingly unaware it was dinnertime.

Reaching for an apron, June tied it around her waist and approached Mary. "What can I do to help?"

Mary paused, then resumed cutting squares of piping hot corn bread. Brushing a lock of hair off her forehead, she pointed the tip of the knife at a pile of plates. "You can get the children started."

"That sounds like a job I can handle."

June turned to see Parker filling the doorway, looking very big, and very out of place in a kitchen. She smiled. "You want to start with the smallest ones first?"

Parker picked up a plate, studying the heaping bowls of mashed potatoes, green beans, turnips, carrots, fried apples, sweet potatoes, and a myriad of other dishes lining the table.

"Fill their plates as you would your own." June handed him a heaping platter of golden brown fried chicken. "But remember, they don't eat as much as you."

Parker grinned. "Nobody eats as much as I do."

When the plates were ready, June and Parker corralled the children to a corner table. The kids began to eat, methodically swallowing as if they barely tasted the food. June noticed the younger ones' eyes occasionally searching the room. How they would miss Angeline.

Simon insisted on feeding the youngest child, who was delighted to have the honor of sitting on the big logger's lap.

Once the children were settled, June drew Sam aside. It might be too soon to discuss the matter, but it weighed on her mind. Steering her friend into the kitchen, June threaded Sam to the far end of the pantry, where they could talk in private. "Sam, is Joe going to stay on and help with the children?"

Freckles stood out on Sam's pale features. Her eyes were red from weeping. "I'm not sure, lovey; I haven't been about askin' 'im, yet." She walked to the small window and stared out. A heart-wrenching sadness filled her voice. "I suppose he will. . . . I just assume he'll be stayin'. Ain't like he's got a bloomin' lot of places to be goin' . . . if you know what I mean."

June nodded. The orphanage was the only home Joe had known for many years. He was an old man now; starting over would be difficult.

"If he's not set on stayin' . . . suppose I could send for me mum. . . . But she's up in years herself. As white headed as the snow on them mountains. Done raised her family, she has. And a second one as well, what with me bein' born so late in life. Don't think she has the energy to take on all these kiddies." Sam wiped her hands on her faded apron. "No . . .

wouldn't be right to ask me mum to do such a thing. Would be the death of her, I'm thinkin'."

June chose her words carefully. Papa had always said, "Say what you mean, and mean what you say, lest you live to regret it." That's how she tried to live her life: meaning what she said. "Well, regardless of whether Joe does or doesn't stay, you're going to need help."

"Ow, that be the gospel for sure. No blasphemy intended." Sam's words faded to a whisper. "But I'll tell you this, June Kallahan: I'll be doin' it meself if necessary."

"Sam, that's a frightening responsibility for one person to assume."

The familiar spit-and-vinegar spirit Sam ordinarily possessed suddenly bloomed with a vengeance. "I'll not be shippin' them poor kiddies off in a million different directions! They may not be me blood kin, but they're family. *We're* family. And we'll stay a family no matter what."

June grinned. That's what she wanted to hear! The old Sam was back. "And I'll be right beside you," she declared.

Sam blew her nose. "You're a good

woman, June Kallahan.'' Her thin shoulders trembled beneath her thin dress. ''Sorry I'm so blessed testy. I should've known you had somethin' up your sleeve. But, me dear, dear friend, you've already given so much of your free time helpin' out 'round here. Not to mention time making those pretty necklaces so the kiddies can have shoes and peppermint sticks. You got your responsibilities with the crusade, and Sunday services at the loggin' camps. I don't see how you can manage to spare another hour.''

''Don't worry about me. I can fit in a lot more when it comes to the Lord's work.'' June met Sam's teary gaze. ''I've been thinking. I want to help more around the orphanage—and I could, if I spent less time traveling back and forth.''

Sam wiped at her eyes. ''I expect that's true.''

June gently squeezed Sam's hand. ''The complex is old and drafty. So is the orphanage, for that matter, so I wouldn't be any better off there than here. I want to stay here awhile—if you'll have me.''

''Have you?'' Sam started laughing and crying at the same time. ''I'd be plumb off me bean to refuse the offer! Oh, June. The kids love you so. And you're the best friend I've ever had. A sister to me, you are. A real sister. Of course I'll have you!"

"Then it's settled. I'll move in first thing tomorrow morning."

"Me prayers have surely been answered!"

"What prayers?" June teased. "I thought you didn't like all that praying."

"Out loud, lovey. When I be by meself, me and the Lord have jolly good talks."

June was proud of the progress Sam was making. It was the Lord's doing, but she liked to think she had a small hand in it.

"Sam, I know sometimes it doesn't always feel like it, nor do circumstances always go according to what we want, but God answers prayers. In his own time and in his own way—sometimes he says yes; sometimes he says no; sometimes he says wait. But always, always, Sam, he answers us."

"I know he surely does, lovey." Sam playfully pulled June's nose. "Lord knows he's makin' me see that more and more lately."

June spotted Joe standing outside the kitchen doorway. "Do you think Joe would mind helping me fetch my things from the complex?"

"I'm sure he wouldn't." Sam frowned. "But what about Reverend Inman? What's he gonna think about all this movin' about?"

June toyed with a loose strand of hair, avoiding Sam's anxious look. What *would* Reverend Inman think about her moving into the orphanage? She didn't want to hurt his feelings, and she would work just as hard or even harder for the crusade. Sam desperately needed her help, and other than counting money and collecting donations, she wasn't really needed at the complex. She could be at nightly services; her job with the ministry would be unaffected. How could Reverend Inman object to her helping a friend in need?

Sam's hazel eyes widened with disbelief. "You mean you haven't talked with him about movin' in with a bunch of bloomin' ragamuffins?"

"You're not ragamuffins!" June chided. "Besides, it isn't like I've deliberately kept anything from him. I really haven't had a chance to talk to him. He isn't a monster, Sam. He'll recognize the need and insist that I help out."

"He'll throw a tizzy fit, he will." Sam shook her head. "He might be a godly man, but he's a stubborn one, wearing horse blinders when it comes to that tabernacle. He'll be hurt, he will."

A rush of pity washed over June. Her decision to move into the orphanage probably *would* hurt Reverend Inman's feelings. After all, he'd been gracious enough to take her in after Eli's death. But surely he would understand her motives, especially now that Aunt Angeline was gone.

"Reverend Inman will understand. He will consider the circumstances and agree that it's the only Christian thing to do."

Sam eyed her skeptically. It was easy to see she didn't agree with June's logic.

"Oh, stop worrying. If my decision bothers him—well, I'll just have to cross that bridge when I get to it."

"You best be mindin' your crossin' and don't go fallin' off that bridge," Sam cautioned.

"And what's that supposed to mean?"

"The reverend has a way—how do you Yanks say?—a way of wantin' his own way. Just like a man, eh, lovey?"

"Reverend Inman would never try to talk me out of doing charitable work," June defended.

"Maybe. Maybe not. But if it comes down to you not bein' as involved with the crusade—"

"It won't. My work with the crusade won't be affected. I'll make very sure of that."

Sam's silence was more eloquent than any words.

June's impatience surfaced. "Everyone seems to think the tabernacle is all Reverend Inman is concerned about. It isn't. He cares about his flock—about his people." June was suddenly trembling, and she didn't know why. Parker, and now Sam, had implied that Reverend Inman was blinded by greed.

Sam patted her hand. "Maybe I'm bein' a tad hasty. Who am I to judge the reverend? You know him better than anyone, what with the time you spend with him."

"I do, and I've seen how he works from daylight to dusk, down on his knees day after day, praying for guidance. Everyone connected with Reverend Inman wants to see the tabernacle raised. But that doesn't mean we aren't allowed to carry on God's work in other ways."

"You don't need to convince me," Sam assured her with a warm smile. "I may not know Reverend Isaac Inman, but I know *you* like the back of me hand. You wouldn't defend anyone not worth defendin'."

"Thank you, Sam." June got so heated when she talked about the tabernacle. She was tired of defending it and Reverend Inman.

"I knew the very day we met on the steamer that our friendship was a keeper."

June laughed softly. "Kindred spirits, that's what we are. Everything happens for a reason, Sam. Nothing happens by chance. The Lord brought our paths together for a specific purpose."

Sam added with a serious note, "You've certainly been a godsend to me and the children."

It was nearing dark when the last wagon rolled out of the orphanage yard. June stayed to clean up while Sam put the children to bed. Parker was one of the last to leave, offering June a ride back to the complex. She thanked him but declined his offer. His day had started before sunup. By the time he waited around for her to finish, took her to the complex, then rode back to camp, it would nearly be time for his new day to start.

Reverend Inman stopped by the kitchen to offer his assistance. June expressed her gratitude but insisted he go ahead, explaining that she wanted to keep Sam company for a while.

Part of her reason was that she wasn't ready to discuss her plans with Reverend Inman yet. She needed time to digest her decision, think it through, prepare a valid argument.

When she defended Reverend Inman, she meant what she said. He was caring, and giving, and concerned about others. But some of what Sam contended was true as well. Reverend Inman could be very persuasive when he wanted. It wasn't that she was afraid he'd talk her out of moving to the orphanage; she had her mind made up about that. She just didn't want a confrontation, especially after the emotionally draining day.

The rain had stopped, and a cold moon hung low in the sky when Ol' Joe stopped the wagon in front of the complex. The Indian waited until she was safely inside, then waved and drove away into the night.

Stretching out across the bed, June closed her eyes, her head swimming. The day had been long and difficult.

Eventually she rose, changed into her flannel gown, then said her prayers. *Lord, help the children. . . .* She fell asleep before she could complete her train of thought.

The sun was peeking over the horizon when she awoke, feeling as tired as when she'd gone to bed. Quickly she washed and dressed, then set about packing her few belongings.

She spread the worn patchwork quilt on the single bed and fluffed the pillow, stood back, and then rearranged them, realizing she was procrastinating.

You're being silly. Reverend Inman will be awake now. Go to him, tell him your plans, share breakfast with him, then ask him to come with you to the orphanage— possibly spend the day with the children. Ol' Joe will be coming soon. She had no reason to feel such dread. What she was doing was right. The children needed her. And it wasn't as though she would be neglecting her other responsibilities.

She'd delayed the inevitable as long as she could. Even at this early hour she knew exactly where to find Reverend Inman. He would be in the revival tent, absorbed in his morning devotions. Leaving the complex, she hurried to the tent.

Reverend Inman was kneeling at the altar in prayer. He started each new day in the same manner before preparing the subject of his nightly message. June slipped into the front pew to wait.

When Reverend Inman finished and stood up, he looked around, and a quick smile crossed his face. "June. I didn't expect to see you up and about so early. You must have stayed at the orphanage quite late. I listened for your return, but I was overcome by exhaustion."

"It was late when Ol' Joe brought me home."

Tight lines around Reverend Inman's eyes made him look older this morning. June worried that he wasn't getting enough rest.

He nodded. "I'm told we can expect another large crowd tonight."

"Praise God."

"Yes, indeed. Praise his name. Seems there's a new logging camp not far from the grounds. As unusual as it is, most of the men have brought their families with them. The foreman rode out just yesterday, and we had a pleasant visit. Said he'd heard about our revival all the way to Portland. He's excited about joining us in worship and promised that others from the camp would be accompanying him."

"That's wonderful, Reverend."

"Yes, it's exciting to know God's work is being recognized throughout this great land."

"Reverend Inman." June cleared her throat. She needed to get this over with. "I have something I need to tell you."

His smiled faded, and he suddenly looked very old. Shoulders slumped, he sank to the bench. "I suspected as much. You're leaving me, aren't you?"

"No, no, Reverend, I'm not leaving
you."

"No, I know you are. I've been expecting this."

June knelt beside the pew, wanting to
ease the terrible pain creasing his face.
"Reverend Inman, now that Sam's aunt is
gone, she can't care for all those children
by herself. Even if Ol' Joe stays on, the
responsibility is too much for her." She
paused, and the silence was deafening.
"I'm moving to the orphanage."

Sadness played across his face. It
seemed an eternity before he spoke. "You
want to live at the orphanage?"

"Yes. Sam desperately needs my help.
Ol' Joe is old and not able to keep up
with the younger children."

"But you're needed here. You give the
orphanage hours of service each week."
Reverend Inman ran his fingers through a
rim of silvery gray hair. "I don't understand. Why would you want to abandon
Eli's work? Have you forgotten your calling? Have I been unkind—insensitive?"

"No, you've been wonderful, but I am
called to do the work of the Lord—"

"Yes!" His voice lost its timidity and

swelled with conviction. "And the Lord's work is here! Have you forgotten the tabernacle?"

No, she hadn't forgotten the tabernacle, but at times she wished she could. For just one sane moment, she wished she could forget the madness, the sense of urgency that consumed them all. "I'll contribute no less time—"

"Oh, child! You can't *contribute;* you must *commit*—completely and wholeheartedly commit—to this endeavor. Your every effort *must* revolve around its completion!"

"Reverend Inman, building the tabernacle is my vision as well as yours, and it was Eli's. But I feel the Lord has also called me to help care for those children. They have no one but Sam."

Reverend Inman buried his face in his hands. His shoulders shook with emotion. "I cannot believe I'm hearing this. Has Parker influenced your decision? He doesn't approve of the tabernacle—is this your reason for leaving?"

"No, Reverend. Parker doesn't know about my moving. I only made the decision late yesterday afternoon."

Shaking his head, Reverend Inman stared at the altar. "I can't begin to tell you how disappointed I am."

"But you needn't be." June wanted desperately for him to understand. "I'll spend just as much time with the crusade. Moving to the orphanage won't alter my dedication. I'll still collect donations at The Gilded Hen, and I'll stay late after the services—"

"No," Reverend Inman murmured. "No. It won't be the same. Eli had complete dedication to the project. You—you will be pulled in a different direction."

"I don't mean to hurt you," June said, feeling sick to her stomach. She didn't want it to end this way.

"No." Reverend Inman straightened. "I'm sure you don't. Go, go to your orphanage. Eli's dream will live on, with or without your commitment."

"Please, Reverend. I promised to help Sam only until other arrangements can be made. In the meantime, my work with the crusade will continue. I promise you, I'll be just as dependable as ever. My enthusiasm won't wane. Nor will the vision of the tabernacle diminish in my heart."

Reverend Inman released a weary breath. "I can't hold you here. You must do what you feel best."

June stood up, her legs trembling beneath her. She'd expected his disappointment; she had not expected his condemnation. Why must he and Parker see only black and white?

Hanging her head, she said softly, "I'll be moving my things this morning."

The reverend appeared to succumb. He sat quietly, looking at nothing. "I'll have Ben hitch the wagon."

"Thank you, it won't be necessary."

Reverend Inman looked up, as if to confirm her insanity.

"Ol' Joe's coming back for me."

Reverend Inman nodded. "Ol' Joe." Hurt rang hollow in his voice. Guilt gnawed at June. She was torn between loyalty to Reverend Inman and devotion to Sam. If Reverend Inman only understood that she wasn't choosing, that she truly could do both well. "I think I hear Ol' Joe's wagon now. I'm sorry if I hurt you. I never meant to."

Reverend Inman turned away. "You mustn't keep Joe waiting."

June edged toward the doorway, torn between going and staying. "I'll be at services tonight. Just like every night before and every night to come. You'll see. Nothing will change. I promise you."

Chapter Thirteen

Sunday night services were continuing to draw large crowds. Twenty minutes before the sermon that night, latecomers had to search for an empty seat. Loggers from Tin Cup, Pine Ridge, and Cutter's Pass filled the back pews. June's work in front of The Gilded Hen had finally borne fruit. Familiar faces were popping up.

No matter how many times the congregation heard Reverend Inman preach, each service hummed with anticipation. Whether he condemned sin, warned of the consequences of straying from God, or admonished the worshipers to seek God's guidance in every decision, people were ready to listen, to examine their heart for shortcomings.

Tonight Reverend Inman's message was on the Christian walk: What did God expect of his children? June listened attentively, wondering if Reverend Inman ever listened to his own message. If so, how could he fail to see the catastrophic need less than two miles from his own back door?

After services June counted the offering and entered the total in the ledger. Moments later she let herself out of the tent, closing the flap behind her.

Someone stepped from the shadows, and her heart flew to her throat.

"Don't be frightened. It's Parker. I didn't mean to scare you."

"Parker!" She drew a steady breath, trying to get her bearings. "What are you doing here this late?"

"Waiting for you."

He stood in the half shadows. Pale moonlight bathed his face, throwing his strong features into relief. His coat was open, revealing a blue chambray shirt open at the neck. Her pulse tripped erratically. She self-consciously smoothed her skirt. "Is something wrong?"

"No—I just wanted to see you."

Her heartbeat quickened. "You did?"

He smiled, stepping into the light. "If you have no objections."

"No—no objections." She couldn't think of a single one, even if she tried.

"I heard you'd moved into the orphanage. I thought I might give you a ride home. And, what with all the commotion of moving, I wasn't sure you had eaten a proper supper. So I packed us a picnic."

She frowned. "A picnic?" Was he serious? A picnic? At ten o'clock at night? In a million years she'd never have thought of him asking her to go on a moonlit picnic!

"Yeah—I hear you can work up a powerful appetite chasing little tykes around."

She bit back a grin. This was an impetuous side of Parker. He was full of surprises. "Well, they sure can wear a body out."

"Then let's let you relax some."

Parker drew her in front of him, his hand warm in the middle of her back as he guided her toward a waiting buggy. Lifting her into the carriage, he stepped in behind her as she settled her skirts.

"Comfortable?"

"Very—thank you."

"Are you warm? Nights can still be pretty chilly."

"I'm fine." She leaned close, her face only inches from his now, playfully whispering, "Now, will you stop fussing over me, and let's see what you've got in that picnic basket."

He quirked a brow. "Getting pretty sassy, aren't you?"

She grinned. "Sassy and stubborn. That's me!"

Flipping the reins, Parker set the buggy in motion. She longed to ask what had brought about his sudden good humor, but she didn't want to break the spell. Whatever it was, it was fine with her.

Moonlight washed the landscape, the pines casting gentle shadows across the road as the horse trotted by the river. It was a perfect summer night. Stars overhead, a cool breeze. "It's beautiful," June said softly.

"Yes, it is."

"Have you lived in Seattle all your life?"

"Not yet," he confided with a wink. "But I was born not far away."

She shivered against the cool breeze, and he leaned closer, drawing her into the warmth of his arm. She looked up at him, surprised, afraid to move for fear he would abandon the idea.

"Is this better?"

She smiled, snuggling closer. "Much better."

"I could drive you straight home to the orphanage, but I was thinking that perhaps you might want to see a spot that Eli and I often enjoyed. It's here by the river. If you're not too tired."

She didn't feel the least bit tired. "The river?"

"Yes, Eli and I used to go fishing here." A mischievous gleam showed in his eyes. "How would you like to try your hand at fishing?"

"Fishing?" The man was still full of surprises!

"Yeah—I hear they're biting."

"Nothing I like better than fresh panfish."

"Then let's go catch some."

Twenty minutes later Parker stopped the

carriage beneath a bare oak and lifted
June out of the buggy. Taking a feed bag
from beneath the seat, he slipped it over
the horse's head.

June wandered down a small incline,
following the sound of running water.
Moonlight played on the gurgling stream,
making pretty diamond-shaped patterns
on the water.

"I brought something to sit on," Parker
said when he joined her. He spread a
heavy blanket on the ground and set a
basket at one corner.

"What's in the basket?"

"Supper." He grinned. "In case you're a
bad fisherman."

She suddenly felt flirtatious, lighthearted. "Is that a challenge?"

"Didn't your papa warn you not to wager?"

She laughed. "Yes, I do believe he mentioned that one or a hundred times."

Parker handed her a baited fishing pole.
"I can even be persuaded to bait this for
you."

"Such a gentleman," she teased, but
thankful for the offer. The thought of

threading a hook through a worm's en-
trails didn't excite her.

Sitting down on the blanket, she
watched the cork on her fishing line bob
in the water. Fishing had never interested
her. Long hours spent waiting for a poor
fish to bite seemed a waste of precious
time. She would rather talk—have Parker
tell her about himself.

They sat side by side, sharing a quiet
camaraderie. For the first time in a long
while she felt at peace.

This new side of Parker was nearly as
disconcerting as it was pleasant. In her
wildest fantasies she would never have
imagined this man capable of planning a
lovely late-night picnic by the river.

They'd argued about Reverend Inman's
plans, disagreed over his motivation,
mourned Eli's passing. She had alternately
been angry with him—accused him of
having a blind spot when it came to Reverend Inman—and had been drawn to his
strength, to his dedication to Eli, to his
ability to keep a hundred or more lumberjacks in line with a mere evenly modulated
command.

One side of Parker she hadn't experienced was fishing with him. And now, here she was, pole in hand, wondering what she was doing here.

"Hungry?"

She hadn't thought so, but, yes, she was hungry. "Yes. What did you bring that's good to eat?"

Parker opened the hamper and set out a tin of soda crackers, a wedge of cheese, and a plate of what looked to be oatmeal cookies. Very dry oatmeal cookies.

"I packed it myself."

Somehow she managed to seem properly impressed. "It looks very—dry."

He produced a pottery carafe. "Fresh water," he said. And a second—"Coffee, in case you get cold."

Handing her a wedge of cheese, he bit into a cracker. "Go ahead—taste it."

She took an experimental bite and was surprised to find the cheese exceptionally good. "Very tasty."

He cut off another slice and handed it to her. She smiled, shifting it to the other hand. A two-fisted eater. That was sure to make an impression on him.

They ate in silence, sitting opposite one

another on the blanket. This was such a different Parker, a side she found extremely attractive.

A side she could learn to love.

Love. A small word that held such enormous implications.

"This is very nice," she commented, reaching for a cookie. She bit into it, watching her cork bob up and down on the rippling water.

"This was Eli's favorite fishing hole."

She took another bite of cookie, looking at him from the corner of her eye. He was lost in memory, thinking back to a simpler time. Lying back on the blanket, she gazed at the sky. It was such a lovely night—millions of stars overhead. Warm enough, despite the brisk breeze. Was Eli watching? *Hello, Eli. You were right. Your friend is nice—very nice.*

"How did you meet Eli?"

Parker laughed, a masculine rumble coming from deep inside his chest, and she thought how comfortable she was with the sound.

"I nearly ran him down."

"You what?"

"I was driving a wagon back into town.

Eli was walking along the road, head down, deep in thought. As the wagon approached him from behind, he stepped out as if he were going to cross the road. I thought there was no way I could keep from running him down."

"Did you?"

"No—he stepped back in time. We laughed about it later, but it could have been serious. Dead serious."

June smiled. "God at work again."

"That's what Eli said, and I couldn't argue it. He came to work for me a few days later."

"So how did you two become such good friends?" she asked.

"Eli had a bad accident—nearly severed a limb. But again, God led us to a doctor who was developing new methods in that field of medicine. I visited him often in the long weeks during his recuperation, and we became close friends. During his recovery, Eli began attending Isaac's meetings and caught his vision. Since he could no longer work in the logging camp, he felt called to join Isaac's staff.

"He told me about his work with Isaac, what he wanted to accomplish. I didn't agree, but we agreed to disagree. We spent our spare time together, talked hours about God, about God's work, about faith. I found Eli to be a man of great faith, and I wanted to have his sense of assurance, his absolute belief that God was at work in his life and in the lives of others. Even mine.''

"You doubted that?"

"Sometimes," he admitted. He gazed at the gurgling stream. "Often. I suppose you don't?"

"Oh, yes, I do. Not my faith, but whether I'm following God's direction and not my own."

"And you worry about that?"

"Sometimes. I think sometimes I'm not doubting God but myself, my ability to discern his direction."

"I think we all worry about that." He drew his line in and rebaited his hook. "I miss Eli."

"So do I." She sat up, resting her chin on her drawn knees. "Sometimes I want so badly to talk to him again, ask him why things happen the way they do. I know it's silly, but I talk aloud—just as if he were here. I knew him so briefly, yet when he died, I felt as if I had lost my husband."

"Yeah—I find myself talking to him every now and then, too. Isaac's name usually comes up."

"Parker." She frowned. "You really are wrong about Reverend Inman. He's dedicated but . . . granted, maybe to the wrong thing."

He made a disagreeable grumbling sound in his throat, and she changed the subject. "Let's talk about Sam. I wish I could be as certain about what I'm doing as Sam is. As soon as she learned of the need at the orphanage, she knew immediately that was where she belonged."

"You aren't sure what you're doing is right?"

"I know it's right, that I'm filling an important need. I just wonder if that's why I was brought here. Eli is dead, so God must intend me for another purpose."

"Well, maybe the orphanage is it."

"Maybe—but still, it seems like there's more."

He grinned. "I don't see you being unsure about anything. Seems to me you know your mind real well."

She made a playful face at him. "Don't tell anyone, but most of the time I haven't a clue what I'm doing. I just go by that small, still voice that says, 'Do something, June, until you can figure out what you're doing.' But Sam needs help, and I'm it for right now."

June lifted her pole to check if a clever fish had stolen her bait. "I don't like it when I'm uncertain. My papa was a preacher. A good one. A pulpit-pounding, hellfire-and-damnation preacher who never wavered. He made me believe that once your course is set you never stray from it. I set my course for Eli, then his dream . . . and now it seems like maybe I should stray from that. I'm not sure how it all fits together—Eli, the tabernacle, and the orphanage."

"How did you meet Sam?"

"On the ship. We were excited to discover we were both coming to Seattle." She set her pole aside. "Strange, isn't it, that both of us were drawn here by outside forces? Her aunt, and Eli. Now they're both gone." She sighed. "But Sam has Simon now."

"Simon's in love. He's a man of few

words, but he's off the deep end with Sam. I wouldn't be surprised if he leaves me and goes to work at the orphanage."

June sighed, rather liking the thought that love changed lives. "Wouldn't that be nice?"

"For Sam maybe—not for me. Simon's my right hand, but if he wants more time at the orphanage, I can arrange it."

June debated whether to ask her next question. But since they were being so candid . . . "Do you suppose this was God's plan all along? Bringing Sam here so she could meet Simon?"

"Do you think your coming here was his plan?"

She glanced away. "What do you think?"

"I think that remains to be seen." He playfully wedged a cracker into her mouth.

Biting into the crisp texture, she mused, "I truly do worry about the orphans' welfare. Sam can't keep them forever."

If Sam had her way, she'd keep them together, but if she and Simon decided to marry, the care and custody of all those children would be too much for a young married couple. She couldn't stay on at the orphanage—the couple would need their privacy. And Simon would have to keep working, to provide food for his family. In spite of what Sam might say, or even Simon, they couldn't be expected to assume such responsibility for the orphanage.

If she could, June would open a new orphanage and work even harder to convince Reverend Inman and others in the community to support her work.

She longed to talk to Faith about the matter. She smiled when she thought about her sister. She'd just received a letter from Faith, who had not failed to mention the number of eligible young men in the community—men of faith, upstanding men, with solid jobs in stores and banks or who owned their own businesses. Gentlemen. Potential husbands, June read between the lines.

The idea of visiting Faith tempted her. Sometimes she thought she should go—pour out her problems and have a good cry. But then she'd look at Parker, and Sam and the orphans, and she wasn't so ready to go.

"This is very nice. I'm glad you thought of it."

"It's been a long time since I enjoyed a pretty woman's company." He turned to look at her. Moonlight softened his features. "Thank you for remembering my birthday."

She reached over and laid her hand over his. "You don't have to thank me. No—actually, you should be grateful," she amended. "The hand warmers could have been a necklace." She grinned.

Sobering, she gazed at him, refusing to look away. Leaning closer, he kissed her lightly, and it seemed as natural as rain.

"Thank you for the picnic," she murmured.

"Thank you for the hand warmers." He kissed her again softly, on the nose, then on her forehead. "Can I tell you something?"

"Anything."

"You're a lousy fisherman."

She swatted him on the shoulder. "I know. Why do you think I avoid it like the plague?"

How could it be that just a short time

ago she had thought this wonderful, perceptive man was such an oaf?

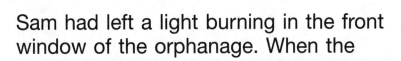

Sam had left a light burning in the front window of the orphanage. When the buggy rolled to a stop, it was very late.

"Thank you for sharing your supper with me."

When Parker didn't immediately respond, June reached over, turning his face to meet hers. He looked at her, and she had the feeling that he was trying to decide what to think about her. But apparently he couldn't decide.

Brushing the backs of his fingers against her cheek, he smiled. "You may not fish worth a hoot, but you're good company." His gaze softened. "Thank you for having supper with me."

Looking into his eyes, June felt a sense of rightness—that Parker was her destiny, even if he didn't know it yet.

Chapter Fourteen

Isaac Inman was tired. Services were still hours away, yet there were Scriptures to review, final preparations for tonight's sermon. He was usually cognizant of the familiar hustle that preceded other services, but tonight . . . tonight he was just too soul weary to notice.

Settling himself at the table, he waved aside Ettie's offer of tea and scones. "I'm not hungry . . . but thank you, Ettie. You're a good woman."

"You work too hard, Brother Isaac." Ettie brought his slippers and adjusted the damper on the stove.

"I'm fine, Ettie. I'd like to be alone."

"Of course, Reverend."

The door closed, and Isaac bowed his head, praying for God's guidance for the evening sermon. When he finished, he opened the Bible to Psalm 32:8.

A familiar peace settled over him as he entered into God's Word. "I will instruct thee and teach thee in the way which thou shalt go: I will guide thee with mine eye."

"Oh, Lord," Isaac whispered. "This is all I ask of thee. Show me, Father. Show me what you would have me do."

The passage so moved him that he slipped to his knees in prayer, giving thanks and praising God's holy name. Rising again, he sat back down.

Every bone in his body cried out for rest. Removing his wire-framed spectacles and faded black jacket, he rubbed his eyes. Was there time for a short nap before services? Perhaps. The mantle clock sounded five soft, melodic chimes as he crawled into his bed and pulled the soft down coverlet to his chin.

His body surrendered easily to sleep, and yet he tossed and turned, thrashing about on the cot.

When he woke, he sat up with a start.

Looking around the small room, he felt confused.

Rolling off the bed, he hurried down the corridor, around the corner, and returned to his desk. Turning to Matthew 5:1-16, he read the Scriptures aloud, savoring the words as if he'd only just heard them.

"And seeing the multitudes, he went up into a mountain: and when he was set . . ."

It was a full thirty minutes later when he prayed for guidance and finished the Scripture.

"Neither do men light a candle, and put it under a bushel, but on a candlestick: and it giveth light unto all that are in the house. Let your light so shine before men, that they may see your good works, and glorify your Father which is in heaven."

When he was finished reading, he closed the book. He sat for a long while, staring into the fire's slow-burning embers.

Finally he reached for a silver bell and rang it.

Ettie appeared momentarily.

"Yes, Reverend?"

"I'll have that tea now, Ettie."

"Yes, Reverend . . . will you be wanting your supper too?"

"No. Just tea. Thank you, Ettie."

~

June arrived at the tent a little before six. She'd driven the orphanage wagon. Sam and Joe thought it best to keep the children home tonight. One of the younger ones was running a fever.

She tied the horse to the hitching post, where Ben Wilson was waiting to escort her into the crusade.

"Evenin', Miss June." Ben smiled.

"Hello, Ben." June gave him a quick hug. "It's good to see you again. I've missed you."

"Yes, you missed me!" Ben giggled.

"I haven't seen you at the orphanage for a few days."

Ben hung his head. "Ben misses you." He perked up again just as readily. "The people here, they need me!" He thrust his chest out proudly as they entered the tent.

June was relieved to see that the service was going to be packed again. Every pew was filled to capacity. Men and women were milling around outside the tent in a standing-room-only crowd.

By six-thirty, songs of praise filled the air. Young and old alike clapped in rhythm to the powerful message found in the music.

Gazing out on the audience, Reverend Inman lifted his arms, commanding silence.

The noise subsided, and every head bowed.

The silence stretched. Finally, in a compelling voice, Isaac said, "Father, we gather tonight to praise you!"

At first, Reverend Inman seemed in command, but as the service wore on, June noticed a change. He seemed preoccupied, searching passages from the Bible as if he were speaking more to himself than to the congregation. Even his demeanor was different. His intense blue eyes skimmed the worshipers, yet he seemed to be oblivious to them.

Gone was Reverend Inman's familiar fiery message. No raised shouts, no prowling the altar, no raising his arms toward the heavens as he preached.

June became concerned. Was he ill?

His features were pale, and he looked tired—incredibly tired. Guilt assaulted her. Was she responsible for his fatigue? In the weeks she'd been gone, she'd worked as hard as ever for the ministry. Only yesterday three loggers had donated an entire month's salary toward the tabernacle.

Reverend Inman's voice drew her back.

"If the congregation will turn with me in their Bibles to Matthew, chapter 25, verses 29 through 46."

The rustling of turning parchment filled the huge tent.

Standing behind the pulpit, Isaac put his spectacles on. "Earlier I prepared a sermon . . . but God has led me to deliver a different message."

Silence prevailed. Every eye steadied on the reverend.

Reverend Inman cleared his throat and began with an uncharacteristic softness. "For unto every one that hath shall be given, and he shall have abundance: but from him that hath not shall be taken away even that which he hath."

He paused, and June saw tears well in his eyes.

"For I was an hungred, and ye gave me

meat," he read softly. "I was thirsty, and ye gave me drink: I was a stranger, and ye took me in."

There was a faraway look in his eyes, and Isaac ignored the tears that streamed down his cheeks.

"Naked, and ye clothed me: I was sick, and ye visited me: I was in prison, and ye came unto me."

Still not referring to the Bible open before him, he continued.

"Then shall the righteous answer him, saying, Lord, when saw we thee an hungred, and fed thee? or thirsty, and gave thee drink? When saw we thee a stranger, and took thee in? or naked, and clothed thee? Or when saw we thee sick, or in prison, and came unto thee?"

Isaac looked up, openly weeping now.

"Verily I say unto you, Inasmuch as ye have done it unto one of the least of these my brethren, ye have done it unto me."

Reverend Inman closed his Bible.

Not a sound was heard throughout the tent.

The ushers exchanged questioning looks. Ben got up and hurried to distribute the offering baskets.

"If the ushers would please return to their seats," Isaac commanded softly.

The activity ceased. The men sat down. Ben looked confused but obediently returned to his bench.

Isaac focused on the congregation, tears rolling down his cheeks. "Tonight it would give me great pleasure if we would stand as a congregation and give thanks for the countless blessings already given in the Lord's precious name."

A man got to his feet, then a woman, then two men. One by one, from all over the tent, the worshipers stood in prayerful gratitude.

What is troubling Reverend Inman? June wondered as she rose from her seat. The service had taken on a surreal atmosphere.

She gradually became aware of sounds outside the tent, and she strained to hear. Was it thunder that shook the earth beneath her? One by one people in the congregation heard the commotion and lifted their heads to listen.

It was the sound of rapidly approaching horses. The hoofbeats were muffled at first; then they shattered the stillness, followed by men's raised voices.

"Fire!"

"The orphanage is burning!"

"Help! Come quickly—there'll be nothing left to save!"

June raced from the tent, threading her way through the crushing crowd. Outside she could smell the deadly smoke.

"Ben!" she shouted.

"Miss June!" Ben was suddenly at her side, eyes wide with fear. "Please don't go. You'll be hurt!"

June raced breathlessly toward the wagon with Ben trailing a few feet behind. "Unhitch the wagon. I can get there faster on horseback. Ben, quickly! Please!"

Ben passed her and quickly unhitched the quarter horse. He picked June up and swung her lithely onto the animal. It was the first time June had ever ridden bareback, but there wasn't time for a saddle.

"Ben—Ben," Ben struggled to get the words out. "Me—me—me come, too! I—I—I can help! You need me!"

June glanced at the orange glow along the horizon, then back at Ben's earnest gray eyes. The orphanage needed all the help it could get.

June steadied the prancing horse. "Ben, I do need you. Ride to the orphanage, and help carry water."

"Yes, Miss June! Ben carry water!" Ben ran for a horse, reciting under his breath, "Carry water, lots of water. Hot. Fire!"

"Ben!" June shouted above the roar of panic. "Don't go into the house! You carry buckets of water, OK? Just buckets of water!"

Ben nodded, reciting as he climbed aboard the horse. "Just buck—buck—buckets of water!"

Parker and Simon had to be told. The stretch of rutted road leading to Pine Ridge was dark and frightening. Bending close to the horse's neck, June gave the animal his head.

Galloping into the sleeping camp, she rode to the bunkhouse, shouting, "Parker! Simon! Help!"

A breathless moment passed, and she shouted again, "Parker!"

A lantern flickered to life. June watched the bunkhouse door until she saw Parker stagger out. Roused from a deep sleep, he hitched his suspenders over his shoulder.

"June?" He struggled to focus on her. "What are you doing out here at this time of—?"

"Come quickly," June pleaded. "The orphanage is on fire!"

Parker blindly reached for the big brass bell hanging from the bunkhouse rafters.

Within moments lights flickered in darkened windows, doors burst open, and loggers poured out into the cold night.

Pine Ridge was all but deserted, save for women and children, when June led a large contingency to the fire.

Horses galloped through the night, hooves pounding.

Simon rode up beside June. "Where's Sam?"

"At the orphanage! She stayed home with the children tonight!"

Skirting her horse, Simon rode ahead.

When the riders arrived at the orphanage, Sam and the children huddled beneath blankets on the road, tearfully watching the old two-story house go up in flames. Though neighbors, along with Joe, Ben, Isaac, and the men from the congregation, had tried to contain the fire, they were powerless against the flames. All anyone could do was watch helplessly as the fire raged, flames angrily eating up the weathered lumber.

June bit back tears of anger. What would the children do now? Hadn't they been through enough? Was there no end to their misfortune?

"Ow, June," Sam blubbered. "Me old auntie's gone, the orphanage is gone—where is this merciful God that's always so good to everyone—where is he, June?" She pounded June's chest, her voice a raised wail.

"Come on now," Simon said, gently prying her away. "This isn't June's fault, Sam. You know that."

Sam dissolved against him in tears and allowed Simon to lead her away.

Reverend Inman was making his way through the chaotic scene, trying to still the younger children's cries. In the midst of the disaster someone remembered to thank God that their lives had been spared.

"Oh, Parker," June whispered as he appeared at her side. He was covered in soot, his clothes singed from going too near the flames. "What's going to happen to those children?"

Drawing her into his arms, he held her close. The front of his shirt dampened with her tears.

With the fire clearly out of control, Reverend Inman took hold of the situation. He dispersed men to gather up frightened children and load them into waiting wagons.

"There's nothing more we can do," he said. "I'll take them to the complex for the night. Tomorrow we'll make proper arrangements."

June couldn't find her voice. What proper arrangements? The only home they knew had burned. Aunt Angeline was dead. No one wanted the orphans on their hands.

Holding June close, Parker questioned Reverend Inman. "Is there room enough at the complex?"

"Ettie will make room."

"We can take a few back to camp with us."

Reverend Inman looked to June for permission.

"No, they should be together—especially tonight."

"They'll be taken to the complex. Workers are waiting to see to their needs. You and Sam must come too."

June wiped her eyes. The matter was no longer in her control. It never had been. "I'll get Sam."

The men were downcast as they walked away from the charred remains. Ben helped load children into the wagons and cover them with blankets.

As the pitiful caravan rumbled off into the night, whimpers were heard from frightened children as big, gruff loggers held them tightly in their arms and tried to comfort them.

Papa's words thundered in June's head.

There's a reason and due season.

Sometimes he comes through on the brink of the midnight hour.

Nothing is left to chance.

He knows our needs before we ask.

Though he sometimes makes us wait, it's all part of his plan.

Remember, June, as big as our dreams are, they can't compare to what he has in store for us. We can't out-dream him, any

more than we can out-give him. He'll al-
ways give us his best. He's never late,
Daughter. No matter the hour, he's always
right on time.

Kicking a smoldering piece of wood out
of the way, June was assaulted by doubt.
Where was God tonight? Why had he
heaped even more trouble on poor, de-
fenseless children? The strange sense of
faltering belief left a bitter taste in her
mouth.

"What are you thinking?" Parker asked,
drawing her aside.

"That I don't know about God, Parker.
All my life I've trusted, believed that, no
matter what, he was there to look after us.
Why would God let something this unspeakable happen? Haven't Sam and I
fought hard enough just to keep shoes on
the kids' feet and a roof over their heads?
Why did God have to go and burn down
the orphanage?"

"You know, June," Parker said, hesitat-
ing only slightly, "I can understand how
you feel. When God took Eli, it didn't
make any sense to me. But we may not
always understand God's way. We have to
trust that he sees the big picture, and

then say, 'In his own way, God knows what's best for all his children.' "

"Right now I'm finding that very hard to do."

Parker avoided her eyes and went on. "The situation here at the orphanage was impossible. Sam has tried to make a run-down house a home for—how many children? She couldn't run this place alone. She's lost Angeline, and Joe's old. The fight to build that blasted tabernacle and keep the orphans clothed and fed is draining the whole community. With the orphanage gone, the settlement will have no choice. They will have to do something with the children."

June felt her hackles rise. "Why don't you just come out and say what you mean, Parker, instead of reciting all these nice platitudes?"

Parker sobered. "I've said what I mean. You're not thinking straight. You can't run an orphanage on a hope and a prayer, June."

"Well, I can, Parker. And I'll fight with every last breath in me to see that those children are not packed up and carted off like some abandoned livestock. They aren't pieces of property! They are God's children."

A muscle tightened in Parker's jaw. "What God?"

She kicked at another ember. "You know I didn't mean what I said a minute ago. I'm just mad at God right now—it doesn't mean I believe for one moment that he isn't here, watching this whole fiasco."

June's emotions were running the full gamut. She was tired, frustrated, heart-broken. When the full meaning of Parker's earlier statement hit her, she seethed.

There was no mistaking his underlying meaning. He wasn't just glad to be free of the orphanage, he was glad to be getting rid of *her.* He knew that the only thing keeping her here was the orphanage. He was feeling pure-and-simple—relief!

He cocked a brow and looked at her. "What?"

June Kallahan, the mail-order bride from Cold Water, Michigan, no longer had a reason to stay in Seattle. In Parker Sentell's hair.

Well, Eli Messenger might be dead. The orphanage might be smoldering ashes.

Her part in Reverend Inman's dream might be over, but she still had her pride. She backed away. Anger left her speechless. She would not let Parker see her cry; she would not! She had foolishly fallen in love with him, and now look what happened.

In love.

The thought hit her harder than Parker's betrayal.

She was in love with Parker; she had been for weeks. Why hadn't she realized it? For some time now, she'd known he wasn't like any other man she'd ever met. He didn't have Eli's sensitivity or easy kindness, but she loved him all the same.

Parker shifted stances, his anger evident now. "Where are you going? Just once I'd like to have a conversation with you that didn't end in a disagreement—June—"

She hadn't realized how slippery the ground beneath her was. Papa's stern, "Pride goeth before a fall," flashed through her mind as she felt her feet fly from under her.

Parker reached out to break her fall, but it was too late. The next thing June knew, she was lying facedown in the mud.

She groaned, clamping her eyes shut in humiliation. Why must she always behave like a bumbling fool in front of him? She rolled to her back to see Parker standing over her, grinning.

"What's so funny?"

"You are." He took her by the arm and set her on her feet. Using his handkerchief, he wiped mud out of her nose. "You're a pretty sight."

June jerked her arm free. "You've made your feelings perfectly clear, Mr. Sentell—stop wiping my nose!" She yanked the handkerchief out of his hand and threw it on the ground. "I don't need your help!"

"You need somebody's help." Parker crossed his arms over his chest and stared at her. "What's wrong with you? Surely you don't blame God *and* me for starting the fire."

Her tears got the best of her. How could he be so nice one minute and so—so blasted infuriating the next? "I don't blame you for anything," she cried. Tears started down her cheeks.

"June—" His stance softened. "What's wrong, sweetheart? Look, I'm sorry about the fire—I'd have done anything to prevent it, but it's over. The orphanage is gone, but the children are alive and well. You should be thanking God instead of accusing him of being in cahoots with me.''

June swung around, searching for her horse. Where could he be? Someone had taken him, or the animal had tired of waiting and headed back to camp on its own. Whatever the reason, it was just more bad luck, the same bad luck that had plagued her from the moment she stepped off the steamer in Seattle three months earlier.

There was only one thing to do. Walk. And she certainly wasn't looking forward to that. It was pitch dark, she had no lantern, and the crusade camp was a long, long way from the orphanage.

Gathering her muddy skirt, she struck out.

''Hey!'' Parker fell into step with her. ''Where do you think you're going?''

''Back to the complex.''

''I don't think so—not by yourself, you're not.''

''Ahh, ahh, ahh! Watch it! You sound concerned, and we both know that's not possible. I can take care of myself just fine, thank you.''

June kept walking without a single look in his direction.

"Is that right?"

"That's right."

"Those are mighty brave words for a woman who can't even find her horse."

"I know exactly where my horse is." June kept walking although at the moment she couldn't see her hand in front of her face and she *didn't* know where that silly horse had gone.

She was suddenly walking alone, and she felt a shiver of anticipation. Well, fine. She'd known he was a cad from the beginning.

In the distance, she heard approaching hoofbeats.

"Give me your hand," Parker said dryly from atop his perch on the stallion.

"No."

"Give me your hand, June. Don't make me get off this horse and put you on this animal."

"Parker Sentell, don't you dare threaten me!"

His snort made it clear he was put out with her behavior. "I'm not going to leave you out here in the middle of nowhere.

And I am not riding this horse behind you as you walk!"

June's footsteps slowed. It *was* awfully dark out here. Something hooted in the distance. And she glimpsed something with big yellow eyes. . . .

She could accept his ride, she reasoned. But she didn't have to talk to him.

"Are you going to get on this horse?"

Glaring up at him, she reached for a hand up. When he hoisted her up behind him, she teetered on the saddle.

"I don't bite," he said dryly.

Catching him around the waist, she latched on. "Well, I do."

He laughed, and touched his heels to the horse's flanks.

She needed time to think and sort her emotions. She must leave Seattle! She must go to be with people who loved her. Family that she didn't have to second-guess all the time. It was time to visit Faith. A weight lifted from her chest. Yes, she would go to Deliverance, Texas, to see her sister and meet her new brother-in-law. She had to get away.

She had had all she wanted of Seattle, and of Parker Sentell.

Chapter Fifteen

June stared at her reflection in the vanity mirror. How had her life gotten so complicated? What seemed like a lifetime ago, she'd sat with her sisters in Aunt Thalia's parlor and felt proud of herself. Proud that she would no longer be a burden to her aunt, proud to be going west to marry an upstanding man who shared her faith. Now here she was, back in her old room in Reverend Inman's complex. Sam was in another area. Townsfolk had agreed to help with the children until arrangements for them could be made.

Throughout the night June had prayed and sought God's counsel. Her mind had exhausted every conceivable option. As darkness turned to dawn, still no word came from the Lord.

By nature she wasn't impatient, nor was she prone to acts of extreme stubbornness. She thought of herself as submissive, forgiving, charitable when needed. She'd carefully considered her next step, and she was left with no other choice. Eli was dead, she had failed Reverend Inman, and Parker gave no indication that he wanted her to stay.

Parker. How she wished God had sent her to Parker—illogical as that seemed. She felt a closeness to him, an attraction she was powerless to understand. Yes, even a deep love.

She must leave Seattle now, before she made an even bigger fool of herself. Parker was a man content to live life alone—he never once indicated she had a permanent place in his life.

Oh, he had been affectionate toward her at times—even, perhaps, teetering on the edge of being loving. But never, not even once, did he suggest she become a part of his life. Except for the moonlight picnic, he had never initiated an encounter with her.

She still had a small portion of her savings left. She would purchase ship passage to San Francisco. From San Francisco, she would board the stagecoach that would take her to Deliverance. She'd be done with the whole unpleasant situation before week's end.

Sam would be disappointed, but she would understand. Now that the orphanage was gone, it was only a matter of days before the children were placed in foster homes.

Reaching for her hairbrush, she drew it through her tangled locks. She was comforted at the prospect of seeing Faith again. They would laugh and talk and try to figure out why June's plans had never materialized. Faith's steadfast belief was exactly what she needed.

She slipped out before anyone was awake and rode to Seattle to purchase her ticket. There was so much commotion at the complex, no one seemed to notice her absence. When she returned, she packed her meager belongings, then took a moment to sit and compose herself, staring at the ticket. The ship sailed at five o'clock that afternoon. There was still time to say good-bye to Sam. Then she could put the past behind her.

Setting her bag by the door, she stepped outside the complex. Joe and Ben were playing with the children, kicking a ball around the empty crusade grounds.

Ettie was trying to keep up with the toddler, who seemed to always be a step or two ahead of her.

Surrounded by baskets of overflowing laundry, Sam was up to her elbows in sudsy water this morning. Three wooden tubs encircled her, and she rubbed the children's smoke-stained clothes up and down on the large scrub board.

"Aye, lovey!" Sam sighed when she spotted June. "What are you 'bout so early this mornin'?"

June forced a smile. She dreaded telling Sam she was leaving. No one else knew—she wanted it that way, hoping to discourage attempts to talk her into staying.

Sam dried her hands and walked to meet her. "Ow—are you angry with me for spoutin' off last night? I didn't mean it, lovey—"

"No, Sam. That isn't it."

Sam eyed June curiously. "So, are you gonna tell me what's bitin' your back, or do I 'ave to drag it out of you?"

"Oh, Sam . . . since when did you become so perceptive?" Tears welled in June's eyes, and she tried to avoid Sam's concerned look.

"Ain't smarts, lovey." Sam patted June's hand. "Just know a saggin' soul when I see one. You tell Sammie what's troublin' you, other than the fire. That's troubling us all."

June glanced at the children, swallowing around the thick lump suddenly crowding her throat. "Coming to Seattle was about the dumbest thing I've ever done!"

"Hey, now! Don't you be talkin' like that! I know things didn't exactly turn out the way you'd hoped. But if you hadn't come, we'd never got thick as thieves!"

"You remind me of Papa, only he used to say 'tight as ticks.'" June dabbed at the corners of her eyes with her handkerchief.

"Ah, thieves, ticks . . . makes no never mind. Thick is thick and tight is tight. We'll always be close—"

"Sam, I'm leaving."

"What?"

"Leaving. I'm going to Texas to stay with my sister Faith for a while—at least until I can determine what God would have me do. There's really nothing left in Seattle for me anymore."

"Oh, June. Me dear, dear friend!" Sam wrapped her arms around June's neck and held on tight. "There's plenty for you to do 'ere. We'll find another house for the kiddies—"

June shook her head. "No, Sam. I thought Seattle was my calling. But look at all the terrible things that have happened since I arrived. Eli's death, the orphanage burning. I no longer feel a part of Reverend Inman's crusade, and he thinks I've lost faith in the tabernacle. I haven't; I still believe, but I also believe in other needs as well."

Sam was silent for a long moment; then she spoke. "Much of what you're sayin' is true. I'll not be denyin' that. But you're makin' it sound like every bad thing that's happened 'as been your fault."

June bit her lower lip, wiping at tears

that refused to stop. "Sometimes I suppose I do feel responsible."

Sam flared. "Well, if that's not 'bout the most ridiculous thing I ever 'eard! I suppose the next thing you'll be believin' is you're responsible for 'angin' the moon and the stars as well! I got a bit of news for you, missy. Good or bad, you didn't 'ave a bloomin' thing to do with any of it. Not everything is of *your* doin'."

June was stunned. Sam had never talked so harshly before. Her words chafed.

"Eli Messenger, God rest his soul, would 'ave died whether you were 'ere or in Cold Water. It was 'is time to go. As for the tabernacle, you know Reverend Inman will see it through, with or without you—or anyone else for that matter. The orphanage was failin' long afore you got 'ere and long afore the fire brought it down. But because of Reverend Inman's generosity, the kids is eatin' better and sleepin' warmer than they ever were before."

"Yes . . . I told you Reverend Inman is a good man—"

"That he be. But we can't keep our

needs dependent upon the crusade's charity." Sam's lips parted with a sly grin.

June eyed her suspiciously. Sam was hiding something, and June had a feeling it was something good. "Are you going to tell me what's behind that mischievous look of yours?"

"Well, I wish you'd come bearin' better news. But still, I'll share me lot with you."

"I could use a bit of good news."

"It's me and Simon," Sam exclaimed, love flooding her words. "The bloke's done asked me to be 'is bride, 'e 'as."

"Sam, how wonderful! Did you accept his proposal?"

"Of course! Told 'im the sooner, the better."

June hugged her and they did a jaunty dance around the washtubs. "Congratulations! I'm so happy for you and Simon."

"Thank ye kindly. Simon is a good soul, and me 'eart is filled with much love for the man. We want desperately to take care of the children. As soon as new quarters can be arranged, we'll work 'ard to give the children a real home. Joe's agreed to stay on. And even sweet Ben has offered to 'elp, 'e 'as."

"That's marvelous, Sam."

Sam's smile died, and her features sobered. "Be more of a hoot if you'd be stayin' on."

"I wish I could, but it's time for me to go." June squeezed her hand. "Truly it is."

"Can't stay even long enough for the weddin'?" Sam chided. "Fine friend you are."

"I would like nothing better, but it would only make my leaving more difficult. I'm leaving today, Sam. This afternoon."

"This very afternoon?" Sam's eyes widened. "You surely can't be meanin' *this* afternoon!"

"It's for the best. But we'll keep in touch. I promise."

"You bet we will. I'll see to that." Sam's voice grew stern. "And what about you and Parker?"

June hesitated, then said quietly. "What about me and Parker?"

"Have you told 'im you're leavin'—this very afternoon?"

"No, why should I?"

Sam shook her head in disbelief.

" 'Cause you're crazy in love with 'im, and you know it!"

June blushed. "And what makes you think that?"

"It's not what I think. It's what every-one, includin' you, already knows."

"Don't be ridiculous."

"Ridiculous? Me? Aye, lovey, you're the one who needs a good dose of reality." Sam's lips thinned. "You've got to tell 'im; got to swallow your pride and tell Parker Sentell how much you love 'im!"

June felt as though the breath had been sucked out of her. "I could never tell Parker that!"

"Sure you could. If you'd pack that pride as quickly as you did your valise."

"But you don't understand—"

" 'Course I do. There's a fire 'twixt the two of you, burns bright as a torch, it does, every time you get near one an-other."

"That's not a fire; it's a facade!" June defended. "It's the only way we can be around each other without arguing."

Sam shook her head. "Nah, it's a fire all right. I know smoke when I smell it."

"Sam, you're not old enough to recognize—"

"Aye, that's where you're wrong," Sam warned. "I know all about love, no matter my age."

Sighing, June conceded, "Maybe in the past, but this time you're wrong."

"And what would it 'urt if I am? Which I'm not," Sam added. "Just tell the bloke you love 'im. Your heart will never be truly at rest, 'til you do. I know 'e feels the same. And if 'e doesn't, what 'ave you lost? At least you'll know for certain."

"You don't understand, Sam. Last night when the orphanage burned, Parker came right out . . ." For a moment, she couldn't speak.

"Yes?"

"Well, Parker came right out and said the orphanage burning was probably for the best. He kept talking about how the responsibilities were draining everyone and now something would have to be done. If he meant that, then he meant he thought it was time for me to go home."

"Ow, I'm sure 'e didn't mean it that way. You're just borrowin' trouble."

"Well, I was there, and I know what he

said. And there's no mistaking what he meant. It was as if he couldn't wait to finally be rid of me."

Sam shook her head. "I think you misunderstood. From what you've told me, it doesn't sound anything at all like the mountain you're makin' it out to be."

"I thought you'd be on my side, Sam!" June burst into fresh tears. "Don't you realize how humiliating it is for me to even tell you about—?"

"Ow, now!" Sam stepped closer to comfort her. The smell of lye soap and wash water swept over June. "I'm always on your side. But I'll always be tellin' you the truth the way I see it. And this time I think you're wrong about Parker and 'is intentions. For the sake of love, I'm beggin' you to go see 'im. Ask 'im straight-out to make 'is feelin's known."

"Sam, I can't do that." She just couldn't. That would just confirm that she was an utter fool. "I understood his remarks all too well. He will be relieved to see me go."

Sam sighed. "Well, I guess there's no convincin' you."

"No, Sam." June wiped her eyes and

put the handkerchief back in her pocket.
"I know when I'm beat. I want to leave
with some measure of my pride intact."

"Would you like for Simon to drive you
to the dock?"

"Thanks, but that isn't necessary. Ol'
Joe will. I'm sure he won't mind." June
paused. "Besides, if Simon took me,
Parker would know. And I'd just as soon
be gone when that happens."

Tears glistened in Sam's eyes. "I'll miss
you."

"I'll miss you, too."

"We'll stay in touch?" Sam's voice
cracked.

"Always."

The women hugged, and June left in
search of Reverend Inman, but she
couldn't find him anywhere.

Joe was next. He was shocked when
she told him she was leaving, but he said
he would be glad to be of service and
drive her to the dock. Ben openly cried
when he heard the news. With her ride se-
cured, June returned to her room, where
she paced the floor and counted the
hours until time to leave.

Each tick of the clock was louder than

the one before. As hard as she tried to rid her thoughts of Parker, his image filled her mind. Sam's words haunted her. What if Sam was right? What if Parker cared that she left? What if he actually cared about her? The thought brought both hope and despair.

In a moment of weakness, June grabbed her cloak. She glanced at the clock. A little over two hours remained before the ship departed. She hurried out the door before she had a chance to change her mind. She found Ben playing with the children.

"Ben!" June shouted as she quickened her steps.

Ben waved. "Hey, Miss June! You come to play with us?"

June frowned. "No, Ben. I need a favor of you."

Ben turned to the children. "Miss June needs me. I'll be right back."

"Ben, could you hitch the buggy for me?"

"No trouble for Ben." He smiled, then sobered. "I will miss you."

"I'll miss you, too." She hugged him, teary eyed.

His sunny disposition returned. "OK!"

Ben quickly hitched the buggy and helped June climb aboard.

"Thank you, Ben."

"Miss June welcome. Ben go play with his friends."

June headed the buggy toward Pine Ridge at a fast clip. Her stomach felt as knotted as a sailor's rope, and her mind raced with every conceivable reaction Parker Sentell might have to news of her leaving. She alternately quaked and prayed as she whipped the horse to run faster.

The buggy bounced along the rutted road, and she reminded herself she was only going to tell Parker good-bye. It wasn't as though she'd had a change of heart. She *would* be on that ship when it sailed at five.

Parker was just leaving the office when June pulled the horse to a stop. He waved and walked in her direction.

She waved back, her heart heavy with the knowledge that this was the last time she'd ever see him. Blast that Parker Sentell anyway. Why did he have to be so good looking? So tall, and so sweet when he wanted to be, so ornery when he didn't.

Why hadn't he fallen in love with her as she'd fallen hopelessly in love with him?

Parker reached the buggy, smiling. "Hello. I was just on my way to check on you and the children. Is everyone all right?"

"Yes—no one seems worse for the wear," she admitted.

"Good."

He smiled, and she faltered. Last night he'd called her sweetheart. The term was apparently meaningless to him, but she had rather enjoyed it and wished he'd said more. A woman, any woman, would be likely to take a remark like that to heart. How could he call her sweetheart in one breath and in the next, wish her gone?

Their moment of truth had come. She prayed that when she explained why she was here, Parker would admit his love and forbid her to go—but she thought that terribly unlikely.

"I . . . I'm leaving." June avoided his eyes, afraid she might see relief written there. Her heart couldn't accept such open rejection.

Parker's smile faded. "Leaving?"

"This afternoon," June said softly. "I'm leaving Washington, and even though you and I never really saw eye to eye on much, Sam thought you should know." She took a deep breath, refusing to meet his eyes. "Sam also thought I shouldn't leave without saying good-bye." She watched the muscle in his jaw tense.

"Sam thought that."

"Yes, Sam . . . and, I guess, I did too."

He took her chin and made her look at him now. "This is kind of sudden, isn't it?"

"No, I've given the matter sufficient thought. The time has come—"

"What do you mean 'the time has come'? And how much thought could you have given it? The orphanage only burned last night."

"There's no longer a reason for me to stay on. With Eli gone, the orphanage gone—"

She flinched as his eyes darkened, and his voice lowered. "Did you ever consider there might be other reasons for you to stay?" Each word was an accusation.

"If you're referring to Reverend Inman's crusade, I'm not needed there any longer either. I still believe in Eli and Reverend Inman's dream for the tabernacle, but deep in my heart I know the Lord will bring that vision to pass without my help."

Parker studied her, his eyes reflecting none of what he was feeling. How could he just stand there and say nothing? She longed to cry out, beg him not to let her go.

The silence was unbearable, his face unreadable.

"Where are you going?"

"To Texas, to be with my sister."

"And you hope to find what there?"

"Peace—a sense of purpose. I've had neither in a long time."

He looked away, as if to sort his thoughts. She bit her lip. Blast that Sam! This was a foolish idea at best. She should have just left and let him find out later that she was gone.

"Well, I need to be on my way." June smoothed her skirt and renewed her grip on the reins. "I—" She blinked back tears. "Good-bye, Parker."

Parker's mouth tensed when he turned

back to face her. "You're sure this is what you want?"

June fought back scalding tears. "Truthfully? I'm not certain of anything anymore."

The moment stretched. Would he let her go so easily? If he did, then he surely didn't return her love.

Finally he took a step back. "I wish you Godspeed."

June's lip quivered ever so slightly. "Thank you. And I pray the same for you."

The buggy started to roll, and Parker reached out to grasp the bridle, stopping the horse. June's heart pounded like a tribal war drum. Every nerved tensed. He didn't want her to go! He needed her in his life as much as she needed him in hers!

"Before you go I have something I need to give you."

Her enthusiasm waned. Of course. Probably her box of Sunday service supplies.

"Wait here. I'll only be a minute." Parker turned and strode through the open office doorway. He was back in a moment. "I want you to have this. I've been meaning to give it to you for a long time now."

June accepted the small burlap sack, having no idea what it contained. "Thank you."

"Go ahead, open it. There's a story behind it. I know your ship is leaving soon, so I'll keep it as simple as possible."

June opened the sack and dumped a single sizable gold nugget into the palm of her hand. "Oh, Parker. I can't accept this. It's far too expensive—"

"It's fool's gold."

June shot him a look of disdain. Was he now implying she was a fool? He certainly had his nerve.

"Well, if it's fool's gold, perhaps you should keep it for yourself." She handed it back.

Taking her hand, he folded it gently around the glistening nugget. His blue eyes confronted hers evenly. "You don't understand. When Eli and I first met, we had big dreams of striking it rich. We went panning for gold every opportunity we got. Tales of other dusters hitting the mother lode abounded. Finally one day, when we were just about ready to call it quits, Eli panned this beautiful nugget. We hurried into town to stake our claim and weigh the nugget we were certain was worth a king's ransom."

June smiled despite her best efforts to keep a solemn face. It was so obvious Parker had loved Eli like a brother.

"When they appraised our good fortune, we quickly found out it was nothing more than fool's gold."

"I'm sorry. . . . You must have been terribly disappointed."

"Yes and no. Seems we were the only panners in these parts to hit fool's gold. But Eli was quick to assess the situation. Said that material riches didn't matter, that only love endured."

"Eli was a wise man."

"Yes, he was." Parker's voice dropped. "He and I kept this nugget as a reminder. Now that he's gone, I want you to have it."

"Oh . . . no, I couldn't—"

Parker squeezed her hand shut around the nugget. "Take it, and think about its meaning."

"I have to be going." June still prayed

for his last-minute confession—anything that would encourage her to stay.

Parker let go of the bridle and stepped back. "Have a safe trip."

"I'll try." June snapped the reins, and the horse trotted on. Hot tears rolled down her cheeks. *Thank you, Lord, for helping me contain them as long as I did.*

Chapter Sixteen

As a cool gray dawn streaked the eastern horizon, Isaac retreated to the solitude of the mountains, something he often did when he was in earnest search of God's answers.

He found a special place of quiet seclusion where he could be alone with the Lord, seeking communion and counsel for his divine purpose in life.

It was late evening when Isaac returned, his heart burdened with unanswered questions.

Ben came running to tell him the sorrowful news. June Kallahan was gone.

Hours ago Ol' Joe drove her to the docks in the orphanage wagon.

"Did she say why she was leaving, Ben?" Isaac asked.

Ben thought long and hard, his face a tight mask as he tried to remember Miss June's exact words. "To visit her faith."

June had gone to visit her sister. "Thank you, Ben."

"Will Miss June come back, Reverend?"

"What did she tell you, Ben?"

Ben's eyes were confused. He nodded his head. "She will come back. Ben knows she will."

"Pray that she does, Ben."

It was past midnight before Isaac finally crawled between sun-dried sheets. As tired as he was, sleep was slow to come. He tossed and turned, throwing covers aside. Toward dawn he was awakened from a fitful slumber.

Climbing out of bed, he reached for his spectacles and hooked them over his ears. Moving to the window, he looked out, trying to see what had awakened him. Dawn was just breaking over the deserted crusade ground. Nothing was stirring but

Ben's old coon dog just coming in from a night of prowling.

His faint reflection gazed back at him from the windowpane, and again he examined his heart. All he'd ever wanted was to glorify God, to give God his best without question or doubt. Had he lost sight of God's will for his life, his ministry? Had the vision of the great tabernacle somehow gone from a powerful edifice for the Lord's work to a personal obsession?

Was he building the tabernacle as a monument for God or for the wife he'd adored for forty years?

Isaac stirred, confused for a moment. Something had brushed his heart. Something light, something intangible, something so sweet and so pure he could have no doubt about its source.

God had just made his presence known.

Tears rolled from the corners of his eyes, and he knew. Knew with crystal clarity that his intentions were pure but somehow he had been obsessed with the tabernacle.

He had misinterpreted God's instruction.

The sermon he'd begun the night the orphanage burned resonated in his mind.

That message, more than any other message he usually preached, held the answer.

"For I was an hungred, and ye gave me meat: I was thirsty, and ye gave me drink: I was a stranger, and ye took me in: naked, and ye clothed me. . . ."

The faces of children appeared before him. Thin faces. Unsmiling faces. The beseeching eyes of orphans asking for no more than the necessities of life.

As the Scriptures and images flooded his mind, he dropped to his knees. *Father in heaven, how could I have been so blind?* His heart was overcome by the shame of it.

He remained in prayer until a knock sounded. He got slowly to his feet and shuffled to answer the door. A grim-faced Parker awaited him.

"We need to talk."

Nodding, Isaac gestured him inside and complied in a soft voice. "Yes. It's time."

⌒

The long passage to San Francisco seemed endless. June spent hour after hour prowling the decks, wondering if she was being too hasty. Should she have stayed longer, given Parker more time to sort through his feelings? He obviously cared for her in his own way. But did he care enough? Now she would never know that answer.

Each time she felt she was making progress at putting the past behind her, everywhere she turned she saw young lovers holding hands, openly displaying their affection. Strolling the deck in the romantic moonlight, they whispered words of love.

On this voyage there was no Sam to give her a warm smile and a comforting hug. No Sam to share cookies and tea. No Sam, period. Sam was with Simon, and June was happy about that. Though it had been only a few days since they said good-bye, she already missed her friend terribly.

Ensconced in her misery, June sought refuge in her small cabin, hoping that behind closed doors she could somehow come to terms with her loss and her questions. But she sat on the small bunk, tears rolling down her cheeks, grieving for Sam, for Reverend Inman, for the children, and for Parker, the man she had loved and lost.

When Ol' Joe drove her to the dock, she had prayed Parker would ride up at the last minute with a shout, proclaiming his deep and everlasting love. Plead for her hand in marriage.

But he didn't.

Ol' Joe saw her safely on board, and she'd felt that surely, this being the last minute . . .

Still Parker had failed to appear. As the steamer made its way through Puget Sound, Ol' Joe was the only one standing on the dock, waving back at her perch on the high deck.

She wiped her eyes. She would miss Sam, Simon, Reverend Inman, the children, Joe, and Ben. And . . . Parker. Especially Parker.

Something Joe said to her as they'd arrived at the harbor haunted her. He didn't have a lot to say, but he had repeated the phrase *by and by* several times.

What did he mean by that? *By and by. By and by.* The phrase rolled over in her mind. When curiosity had overcome her, she'd asked him the meaning of his strange chant. She would never forget the wise look in the old man's eyes as he turned to face her and simply repeated, "By and by."

Joe was a man of few words. Anyone who knew him agreed. Yet June felt an odd stirring in her spirit by the simplicity of his response. Something told her it meant more.

She searched her heart during the days of passage, looking for a single explanation for why God had sent her to Seattle in the first place.

Eli's death.

The senseless fire.

The incomplete tabernacle.

Parker Sentell.

Answers refused to come.

When the ship docked in San Francisco, June traded modest comfort for a cramped stagecoach, continuing her journey to Deliverance.

Squeezed between a portly, balding man and a pencil-thin young woman wearing a large hat fashioned from a dozen bright peacock plumes, she stared morosely ahead of her. The conveyance occasionally hit a particularly deep rut, violently rocking the coach. The woman's ridiculous hat fell sideways across her face, and June found herself repeatedly blowing a feather away from her nose.

A new morning found her sitting next to the window. Texas was as different from Washington as night from day. She supposed it was pretty, in its own right. The cows were interesting, with those horns that looked like racks strapped across their heads.

Day after day she watched unfamiliar landscape roll past. One afternoon, she suddenly sat straight up, staring at what looked to be a huge rat in armor scurrying across the road. The animal had to be the ugliest thing she'd ever seen!

Sitting back, she wondered if the odd creature was dangerous. She made a mental note to ask Faith.

Although the coach was crowded, no one seemed to care for conversation. That suited her just fine. There wasn't much she wanted to talk about anyway.

The stage stopped at every pothole in the road—weigh stations, the driver called them. Passengers got off, and new ones boarded. At night June slept in a small, crowded room with others and got up before dawn to start out again.

The long trip passed slowly. June felt as if she'd eaten at least a crockful of dust since the onset of the journey. Just when the cramped conditions became intolerable, the stage finally rolled into Deliverance, Texas.

June scanned the crowd. Her heart soared when she spotted her sister standing between a tall, handsome man and a kind-looking older woman. Faith stood on her toes, wildly waving. She was the best sight June had seen in a long time.

"June!" Faith shouted above the confusion, threading her way to the coach.

When the stage door opened, June climbed out and flew into Faith's arms. A lifetime passed before they found the strength to let go.

"Oh, June!" Faith cried. "You look wonderful!"

June blushed. She looked like the wrath of God, having traveled for days in a bowl of dust.

"Mother Shepherd!" Faith motioned for the older woman. "Come meet my sister June."

June extended her hand, but the kind woman with graying hair was quick to embrace her with a warm hug. "It's so nice to finally meet you, June. Faith has told us so much about you."

"Thank you," June replied, looking at Faith. She wasn't sure what she should call the woman who was her sister's mother-in-law.

Liza Shepherd smiled. "You may call me Mother Shepherd if it suits you."

"I would like that, Mother Shepherd."

Faith latched onto the arm of a tall, handsome man who was standing beside her. "June, this is Nicholas."

June shook her brother-in-law's hand.

"Oh, give him a kiss," Faith ordered. "You're going to love him every bit as much as I do."

Nicholas Shepherd's face turned a crimson red.

June settled for a polite handshake. The kissing would have to come later—much later. "I'm delighted to meet you, Nicholas."

"My pleasure." Nicholas shook her hand, and she noticed his grip was firm and confident, like Parker's. "I'll collect your bag while you ladies catch up on your gossip."

The carriage ride to Faith's home was luxurious compared to the stage. The stylish coach rolled along the verdant countryside with hardly a bump. June listened attentively as Faith pointed out the endless acres and hundreds of cattle that comprised the Shepherds' ranch.

Nicholas halted the buggy in front of a towering two-story house. Various porches held dozens of ferns swaying from the rafters. Colorful flowers bordered the stone walkway. Everything about the Shepherd house reflected love.

Nicholas helped the ladies from the buggy, then reached for June's valise.

"Are you hungry?" Faith asked.

June's stomach knotted as she remembered all that dust. "Not really."

"Well, you will be when you taste my pot roast," Mother Shepherd promised.

"Mother Shepherd, I'll show June to her room; then I'll be down to help you," Faith said.

"Not tonight, dear." Liza smiled. "Tonight you'll spend time with your sister. It's been a long time since the two of you had a moment together. I'll not have you wasting precious time with biscuit dough up to your elbows."

"Are you sure?" Faith asked, excitement dancing in her eyes.

"Absolutely!" Liza headed for the porch. "You young people enjoy yourselves. I'll let you know when supper's ready. Keep an eye out for Jeremiah. He'll be eating with us tonight!"

June glanced at Faith. "Jeremiah?"

"Mother Shepherd's beau."

Nicholas pointed the horse toward the barn, taking a moment to steal a kiss from his wife. Faith grinned and kissed him back.

Turning, she reached for June's bag, and the two women disappeared into the house. "You can't believe how different Mother Shepherd is now compared to how she acted when I first arrived in Deliverance. She's a completely different woman."

"Looks like you and Nicholas have definitely warmed to each other. You two act like newlyweds," June teased, recalling Faith's own earlier trials and tribulations. If only June's had worked out so happily.

"We are newlyweds! And I've never been happier. I've had to teach Nicholas a thing or two though. A month ago he would have died from embarrassment if we kissed in front of his mother. What a difference even a little time makes."

"And love."

"Yes." Faith beamed. "Most definitely love."

"Oh, Faith . . . I am so happy for you." If only June had found the same love in Seattle, with Parker . . .

"Your room is down the hall from ours," Faith explained as she pointed toward a huge oak door. "If you need anything, just call."

June's bedroom was exquisite. The walls were painted a pale yellow. The warm afternoon sun set the room aglow.

"It's a wonderful room, Faith," June said. She was determined to hold back her tears. "I'll be most comfortable here."

Faith gave her a quick hug. "I had Nicholas paint it your favorite color."

"Thank you." June turned in her sister's arms. "Oh, Faith, it's so good to be with you. I've made such a mess of things!"

Faith gently led her to the bed and sat

her down on the yellow patchwork quilt. "Oh my. Don't cry. It can't be that bad. Believe me. You should have seen the mess of things I made when I first tried to fit in here."

June wiped at her tears, recalling the letters Faith had written her in the beginning, expressing her doubts.

"Yes, but look how well everything has turned out for you. You have a loving husband, a wonderful mother-in-law, and a beautiful home."

"I thank God every day. But it wasn't always this way, and it almost didn't happen at all," Faith confided. "Your time will come. I promise. No matter how hopeless things look, when you least expect it, God will deliver a blessing even greater than you can imagine."

June sniffled. "I know you're right. But sometimes the waiting, the not knowing— it's so hard."

"Ah, but those are the times God is teaching us patience and encouraging us to grow in our Christian walk. Without trials we would still be babies, crawling around in the dirt, instead of adults, standing tall and proud."

"It's so good to have a sister like you to hold on to until then," June confessed.

Faith handed her a dry hankie. "Now, tell me everything! I want to know about Parker, and Reverend Inman, the tabernacle, Ben, and Simon, and Sam, and the orphanage. Everything!"

June smiled through her tears. "Are you sure you want to hear everything? It's pretty discouraging."

"Everything."

June told Faith everything she could think of. All the disappointments she'd encountered from the day she stepped off the ship in Seattle poured out. She dwelled longest on Parker Sentell.

Her words were forced at times, bitter at others, but June knew the love and warmth reflected in her heart must show in her eyes each time she spoke his name. Parker.

"I don't understand, Faith." June sniffed. "Why would God send me all the way to Washington and then allow all those horrible things to happen?"

Faith held her close. "You know, it sounds to me as though this Parker

Sentell may have been an integral part of God's plan for you."

June was shocked. "Don't be ridiculous! God isn't cruel."

"I don't think I'm being ridiculous. Just look at you. You're an emotional wreck. You're in love with this man, deeply in love with him."

"Well, Parker isn't in love with me. He's in Washington, and I'm here in Texas, a world away."

"For right now. But Texas isn't the end of the earth. You must bide your time, wait for the by and by."

There was that phrase again. The same phrase Joe had used when he saw her off at the dock.

By and by.

First Joe. Now Faith.

Was God speaking to her through them? And if so, what did he mean?

June had promised to stay no longer than a month, but the Shepherds made her feel such a comfortable part of the family, it would be easy to wear out her welcome.

Mother Shepherd treated her as well as

a mother would. And Nicholas was the brother she never had. June and Faith grew closer than ever, if that was possible. On Mondays June accompanied Faith to the school where Faith taught three blind students. June fell in love with Adam, the youngest. They became the best of friends.

The weeks passed, and June realized her month was coming to an end. She would have to book passage back to Cold Water and Aunt Thalia.

She was down on her knees, weeding the vegetable garden one afternoon when Nicholas returned from Deliverance with a letter postmarked to her. He handed her the envelope, his face solemn.

"I believe it's from your reverend friend."

Nicholas left her alone to read the missive. Several moments passed before June found the courage to open it. Finally tearing into the envelope, she scanned the message.

My dearest June:
I pray this letter finds you healthy and happy in your new surroundings. I

deeply regret we didn't have the opportunity to say good-bye. Perhaps it was not in his plans for us to part. Perhaps his will is that our paths will cross again someday. I would like nothing more. You are truly a woman after God's own heart.

The Lord used your charitable spirit to teach me many important lessons. For this I am grateful, not only to the Father, but to you as well, for your faithfulness in his following.

It shames me to admit though, that as good as my intentions were, somehow I had lost sight of God's will as opposed to my own. All I've ever wanted was to glorify God, to give him my best without question or doubt. But I fear I lost sight of God's will for my life, his ministry. The vision of the great tabernacle somehow went from a powerful edifice for the Lord's work to a personal obsession.

I have prayed for his forgiveness, and Parker and I have made a reasonable peace.

Consequently I've been led to revise the plans for the tabernacle. I will build a more modest church. One with large *quarters in the back for a new orphan-age. I united Sam and Simon in holy matrimony, and they have agreed to stay and help care for the children. Through their unselfish efforts, and with the help of the lumber camps and the crusade, the children will stay together.*

I know the orphanage held a special place in your heart. I could not allow an-other day to go by without sending you the good news and asking you to return to friends who love you. You have a place in our community, an important place. As well as in this foolish old man's heart.

For being such a young Christian, you certainly taught this old preacher a val-ued lesson. My heart will always hold you in great fondness.

By and by, all good things come to those who wait patiently upon the Lord. May his tender mercies and great bless-ings be upon your life always.

In Christian love,
Reverend Isaac Inman

June's eyes filled with tears of happi-ness. She should never second-guess

God. All things work for his glory. Her heart rejoiced in Reverend Inman's good news. She smiled, refolding the letter with a sense of peace.

She *knew* Reverend Inman was a godly man, and now others knew.

There would now be a home for the children, a house of worship that would serve the spiritual needs of many . . . the immediate needs of a few. The Lord had certainly blessed the work of Isaac Inman's hands.

Did Parker know—? She quickly shook the thought aside. Of course he did! She didn't want to even think of Parker.

Kneeling, she jerked a weed from the garden, unaware she spoke out loud. "And this, Mr. Sentell, is for kissing me in the moonlight and calling me sweetheart!"

Yank!

"And this, Mr. Sentell, is for being more handsome than any man has a right to be!"

Yank!

"And this, Mr. Sentell—"

"Ouch."

June froze at the sound of the masculine voice. Not just any man's voice. She would know this voice anywhere.

Wiping a stray lock of hair out of her eyes, she let her gaze slowly travel the length of a long, long trouser leg, looking up, up . . . up to see Parker towering above her. Her heart sank when she realized he'd witnessed every spiteful yank.

Squatting beside her, he met her astounded gaze. Without breaking eye contact, he yanked a weed and tossed it aside. It landed in the pile with the others. "And that, Mr. Sentell, is for letting the only woman you ever loved walk out of your life without attempting to stop her." He stared deeply into her eyes.

June's breath caught as the meaning of his words sank in.

"Oh . . . Parker," she whispered, feeling so ashamed of herself. She had been such a fool. Pride. Foolish pride could be such a hurtful thing. His presence here—he was in love with her, too. She should have recognized that all along.

"Can you ever forgive me for being so—?"

"Wonderful," June finished. She sighed, laying her head against his broad chest.

Her answer had come. She was home now. "Of course. If you can forgive me."

"I love you, June. I should never have let you go that day." His hold tightened. "I won't let you go again," he whispered, stroking her unencumbered hair.

"Oh, Parker! I never wanted to go. I was praying you would stop me—I only left because I was prideful and stubborn and I really thought that's what you wanted."

"What I wanted was to take you in my arms, carry you to Isaac, and make you my wife."

"But you never said—"

He gently touched her mouth with his forefinger. "I've been a fool, and it's almost cost me something very important in my life."

Setting her gently back from him, he gazed into her eyes. "June Kallahan, may I kiss you?"

"I do believe I'd die if you didn't."

Pulling her gently to her feet, he kissed her. The kiss was long and sweet and devoid of reserve. He towered over her, but it didn't interfere with his ability to hold her tightly in his big, powerful arms.

When the embrace ended, he dropped to one knee. "Will you marry me? Come back to Seattle with me—share a life with me?"

"Oh, Parker! So many questions!"

Parker cocked a brow, waiting.

"Yes, yes, and yes!"

"I'm the luckiest man in the world."

"Yes, you are." June grabbed his hand, relieved to have that settled. "Come with me. You have to meet my sister Faith and her wonderful family."

"I've already had the pleasure. How do you think I knew you were out here yanking my head off?"

June looked past Parker to the front porch. Faith, Nicholas, and Mother Shepherd watched the two of them with smiles of approval.

Parker sobered. "Isaac told me he'd written you about the orphanage. I know how much the children mean to you."

"Parker—about you and Reverend Inman—"

"Isaac and I have settled our dispute. We've prayed together, and we realize our mistakes. I was judging Isaac by my Uncle Walt. I've asked Isaac to forgive me.

We're working together to build the new church.''

''I'm so glad.''

''Once we're back in Seattle, I think Simon and Sam might welcome our help . . . that is, until our own babies come along.''

''Our own babies?''

''You do want babies?''

June stared up into the eyes of the man God had so richly designed for her. Only for her.

''By and by,'' she replied, finally knowing exactly what God had been trying to tell her.